I0598022

SEARCHING FOR FIFTH MESA

A Novella of the Southwest
Juana Foust

The Sunstone Press
Santa Fe, New Mexico USA

Copyright © 1979, by Juana Foust

ALL RIGHTS RESERVED. No part of this book may be reproduced in any form or by any electronic or mechanical means including information storage and retrieval systems without permission in writing from the publisher, except by a reviewer who may quote brief passages in a review.

FIRST EDITION

Book Design — Douglas Jerrold Houston
Cover Photograph — Kirk Brooks

Printed in the United States of America

Library of Congress Cataloging in Publication Data

Foust, Juana.
   Searching for Fifth Mesa.

   I. Title.
PZ3.F8266Se [PS3511.08]   813'.5'2   78-31284
ISBN 0-913270-81-4

Published in 1979 by The Sunstone Press
Post Office Box 2321, Santa Fe, New Mexico 87501

1

As she picked her cautious way through colonies of cindery rocks, she felt as if her body was being turned on a barbecue spit, browned first on one side and then on the other. Her legs were beginning to feel shaky, especially the left one, the one she broke that time she lost footing and fell out of Grandma's old cottonwood while trying to rescue Tiger, her cat, who had been treed by Old Cojo.

The unmarked, lavic course was delineated only by the stance of the sun whose mood became more and more oppressive as her tag-along shadow shrank beneath her boots, making it noontime. She hadn't eaten or drunk since morning, but she dared not pause for nuts and cold tea. This was a waterless land where one didn't uncap the water bag except as a last resort. Anyway, she wasn't particularly hungry or thirsty. She was just hot.

Shouldering the fetid pack, she moved ahead resolutely. The accursed heat moved along with her, shimmering tauntingly before her gooey eyes.

Then there came a moment of uncertain grace. A stray cloudlet crossed the path of the sun. The sudden shade triggered a chill, a real teeth-chatterer, proving the lava bed to be at a greater altitude than she had supposed, maybe around eight thousand feet. The shivers quickly phased out, as she knew they would, and she felt fine. In a few seconds the cloud shield moved on across the steamy rocks. Not only was she again hot as a Thanksgiving cook stove, but she began to cough, probably from the abrupt changes in breath temperatures. She coughed until she gagged and her fingers sought the cap of the canteen. But the bung did not loosen. Having been educated the hard way to the sly trickery of drymouth that, like the glittering eye of the serpent, numbs the will to resist, she came to her senses, realizing that come what may, her waning water supply had to be kept off limits until a source of replenishment was nigh.

This not being her first experience with dehydration, she knew what to do. She needed to get hold of a smooth, small pebble. In this area of raw, volcanic regurgitation, a specimen like that would be as scarce as a hen's tooth. But for once luck was in her pocket. Lying in the cool shadow of a nearby rock was a small shard of rock crystal about the size and shape of a lima bean.

She quickly inserted the little stone between her tumefying lips, slipping it under her heavy tongue that at first shrank from, then rejoiced in the delicious coolness that had the taste of an icicle. Once activated, the muscular organ worried the alien pebble, priming the salivary glands, and affording the whole oral cavity, an interlude of salubrity that permeated her entire self.

She felt calm and relaxed now, and her mind freely speculated upon the magnificent reward awaiting at the trail's end. So absorbed she became in her dream of what lay ahead, that the heat, the thirst, and the uglified terrain detached themselves from her unpalatable human condition to become something external to herself.

Then, in a sudden flip-flop from future to past, her thoughts turned to a certain chapter of her youthful autobiography, and pausing a moment in her journey, she closed her eyes and began to read. The chapter concerned a certain Sunday when she was seven.

Grandpa's dugout was the capital of our two-family universe, at that time having a population of only six. (Grandma's sister, Aunt Goldie, had been laid to rest and his brother, Nimrod, and his half sister, Aunt Pet, an off-center artist, both had been read out of the family and had gone separate ways. Cousin Cooter, of course, had not yet joined the clan.)

Grandpa, Grandma, and their grown son, Uncle Jule, lived in a prestigious, forty-foot, shiplap-bonneted dugout that had a privacy curtain you could pull across the back fifteen feet and shut off some folding cots, trunks stacked upon each other, and other stuff.

Mama, Daddy, and I lived in our own little dugout on our adjoining home-stead across the road. I remember that at this particular time Mama wasn't sleeping well and she used to cry out in the night, and not entirely because Daddy was away looking for work—his school having closed due to a lack of pupils. She hadn't had a good night's rest since that night when she thought Tiger, my cat, was curled up on her feet to keep warm. When he got too heavy, she whooshed the quilt to scat him. Then, she saw a long lean critter muscle himself up the dugout steps and slither away in the white plains moonlight. But whatever the complexion of her night, a cheerful voice awoke me in the morning.

"Leaf! Leaf Marie, honey, the lark is up!" Mama's matutinal greeting was one she picked up from Daddy, whose soul was dedicated to poetry—he even wrote some.

Rubbing sleep from my eyes, I pushed the cot quilt back and stood up on the hard, dirt floor. Mama pulled my plaid, cotton flannel nightgown up over my head like she was skinning a rabbit and hung it on a nail on the wall over my bed. Self-conscious of my nakedness, I quickly plunged both arms into my denim apron and backed up to Mama for buttoning. As she tidied me up, she reminded, "Be sure to put on clean drawers. You know what day this is." Of course I knew. It was Sunday. I had been looking forward to it all week.

Our bowls of oatmeal were waiting on the table made from empty goods boxes. I slid into my place and picked up my spoon.

"Eat fast but don't slurp," Mama said. Somehow Mama always was in a hurry. As usual, she ate standing up, like a horse.

As soon as we put our empty bowls down, Mama trudged up the dugout steps—and hollered over to Jule who had already done the milking and was taking the foamy bucket home.

"How's Ma?"

"Ma had a pore night," he called.

"We'll be over as soon as I press Leaf Marie's Sunday School dress," Mama hollered. "It won't take long. The iron's been on the stove since before breakfast."

I worked fast, splashing my hands and face in the tin washbowl, wiping them on the roller towel, running the family headcomb through the tangles in my Buster Brown bob, and fastening the ankle straps of my maryjane pumps. By the time Mama gave the finishing touches to my dotted swiss frock, I was ready to go. With the dress tenderly folded across Mama's arm, we hurried across the road to Grandpa's dugout.

Granny was on her spider bed snoring in snorts with her mouth open. Mama went over to the bed and watched Granny closely for about a minute, then turning away, shaking her head, she commented, "I'll vow, Ma looks waxen. What time did you come in?" she asked her brother, who was shaving in front of the cracked mirror over the washstand.

Without taking his eyes away from his lathered reflection, Jule, who bunked inside or under the wagon, depending on the weather, said, "Pa woke me around midnight to come in—Ma was so restless. When she finally dropped off, I told him to go back to the barn and get some sleep. His back was botherin' him."

Again shaking her head, Mama said, "She sure looks waxen."

Having been warned to keep out of the way, I sat on the bottommost dugout step, keeping offside from the slop bucket because even though Uncle Jule already had poured it out, it still had a bad breath. I was casually aware that Mama was juning around, picking up, straightening up, setting the ironing board up across two chairs so she could press the white shirt Jule had laid out, but my chiefest interest centered on the looking glass. Watching a man shave aroused the same physical curiosity about grown-up stuff that I felt when I saw a woman in the congregation open her shirtwaist during a sermon and with two fingers put a teat into a baby's mouth.

Jule broke the sensuous spell. Without turning his foamy jowels away from the mirror, he commented, "Stricklands took Number 22 to Tiaban yesterday to go to the buryin' of Jimsam's brother. He was found dead as a doorknob by the tracks night before, empty bottle by his side."

The mention of the name "Strickland" woke Granny. "What about that no-account Strickland outfit?" she demanded, clucking her tongue in disesteem, and struggling to sit up.

Grandma acted so fidgety Mama propped her up with a pillow and stroked her forehead. "Like a cup of coffee, Ma?" Granny must have nodded because Mama went to the stove, and pouring a cup of arbuckle, held it to her mother's thin, blue lips. After a few sips Granny waved the cup away. Then, sinking into her goose down pillow and closing her eyes, she began to snore again.

Mama watched Granny for a little bit, and then with a warning finger to her lips signaled that talk should be kept low. Leaving Granny's side, she whispered the name "Strickland," tisking her tongue against its mention.

Young as I was, I knew why. Grandma thought the Stricklands were beneath the Bagbys. She didn't want Jule to go with Opal because her mama was a mail order bride. Granny said that Myrtle Strickland already had been married at least twice when she put the "Object Matrimony" ad and the picture of herself in a peekaboo waist in a Kansas City paper. Granny also claimed that Jimsam would have had to be drunk when he sent her railroad fare to Melrose. But then he was as much of a scalawag as she was. That's what Granny said, and we all knew it by heart.

I also knew that the rest of the family didn't share Granny's opinion of the Stricklands, but nobody said anything. Grandma was a sick woman and they tried not to get her upset.

3

Pretty soon Jule, closely shaved, keen-eyed, and handsome as a rodeo performer reached for the white shirt Mama had just ironed. Poking his hairy arms through the empty sleeves, he decently turned his back to the women folk while he unbuckled his rattlesnake skin belt and tucked his shirttail under his pants. Mama unbuttoned my apron, modestly pulling the dotted swiss frock over my head at the exact time the apron fell at my feet, and I stepped out of it.

Smoothing my Sunday School dress down, patting it into shape, tying the blue ribbon sash into a precise bow, she backed away and looked me over approvingly. "I'll bet you will be the prettiest girl in your class today."

Compliments were life's blood to my childish heart. I knew I was not pretty. I knew the relatives knew it and tried to excuse it by saying, "But Leaf Marie is bright. You should hear her spell Waxahachie—that's where Daddy was born—and you should see her report card!"

Even at seven, I knew my shortcomings. I was skinny, my arms were too long for a girl and my eyes were more gray-green than blue like Mama's. So the compliment made me feel real good. Furthermore, my spirits already had perked up. With the Stricklands away at a buryin', Uncle Jule would not be taking Opal home from church and I would not have to ride home with the preacher's family. I began to sing "Brighten the Corner."

In a muffled voice out of the corner of his mouth, Jule said, "Shut up. You'll wake Ma! Anyway you couldn't carry a tune in a bucket." Granny woke up, of course. Bunching her pillow at her back, she sat up and reached for her gold rimmed specs that were lying on the open family Bible at her side.

"Back up here, Hon!"

Knowing what was coming and dreading it, I held back, my whole small body tingling with embarrassment.

"They're clean, Granny. Just ask Mama. I got them fresh out of the clean clothes trunk. Honest I did. Cross my heart."

But Grandma wasn't moved. "I'll check anyway," she declared, adjusting her specs. "This is the Lord's day."

Stamping my patent leather maryjanes on the hard earthen dugout floor, I cried a firm, "I won't!"

Mama was the boss. "You heard what your Grandma said. Mind her, or Jule will go without you."

Humiliated and defeated, I backed up to Granny's bed. She lifted the backside of my dotted swiss skirt to inspect my drawers, my flour sack drawers whose commercial lettering had only been dimmed, not erased, by trips to the wash pot.

Jule looked up from his task of scraping his nails clean with the blade of his barlow. Devilment danced in his eyes.

"Hot Dickety! 'Hunter's Best Flour, Wellington, Kansas.'"

Bursting into tears, I ran up the dugout steps and out to the horselot.

Grandpa had already harnessed Blackie up to the buckboard and left her tied to the hitching post ready to go. I climbed up to my side of the buggy seat and waited for Jule, plotting my revenge, not realizing, of course, that the immature, child-cruel gesture would place a heavy hand on my conscience that would never completely lift. It was Granny's penchant for cleanliness and Jule's teasing that had created the circumstances, but I forgave them long before I forgave myself for that act of revenge. But back to the story.

4

2

When we got too far along the road for Jule to make me get out and walk back, I tossed my sassy head and chided in sing-song, "Two little weevils in a goober shell, I know something I ain't gonna tell."

Jule didn't pay me any mind, so I persisted in the taunting chant. His curiosity finally became aroused.

"All right, since you are acting so smartalecky, what's eatin' on you?"

"It's something bad about you."

He laughed. "I knew sooner or later Ma would get wind of the tale that's making the rounds about Opal and me, but there ain't a word of truth to it. Sunday night when we was goin' home from services, Blackie turned right instead of left at Monday's Wash, and it was gettin' daylight before we got to the Strickland place. I explained and apologized to Jimsam, tellin' him his daughter couldn't have been safer in God's pocket, and he put his gun away. Besides, I'm no child. Ma ought to realize that, and maybe she could, if she could just get it off her mind that Opal's mama was a mail order bride."

"It's not about you and Opal at all," I said, fiendishly playing my trump card. "It's something I overheard Granny and Mama talking about."

"Little pitchers have got mighty big ears," he reminded me.

"Oh, I didn't mean to listen. Honest! I was making a grass-and-mud pie by the window while Mama was sponging Granny and changing her shimmy. They began to talk. I couldn't help but hear."

"All right, Miss Smarty Pants, what did you hear?"

I had Jule right where I wanted him. I could get even with him and I would not have to lie to do it. "Well, Grandma said the reason she was a sick woman was because she borned you. She said, "If I had never had Julius, I would be a well woman today!"

Uncle Jule bit his lower lip and narrowed his blue-gray eyes in cautious thought. "And what did Ethel say?"

"Mama just said for Granny to lay back and rest. What's done is done and can't be undone."

From the disturbed look on Jule's face, I realized I had hurt him more deeply than I had planned. He just sat there, not paying any attention to the road or anything. The buckboard hit a coyote hole and nearly turned over. He grabbed my sash to keep me from falling out.

Feeling morally responsible for the unhappy turn of events, I sank to my side of the buggy seat and hung my head in despair. I would be eight in three months. I was not a young'un any longer. I knew that by deliberately hurting my beloved uncle I had sinned, and I was frightened of what God or the Devil, or the two of them in cohoots, might do to me. More immediately, I was scared stiff Mama would find out and give me the "whuppin" she often had threatened for the "next time." I suddenly burst out crying.

Jule halted the buggy and looping the lines around the whipstock, wiped my tears with his bandana.

"I'm a bad girl," I whimpered between sobs. "I made the whole thing up."

"Hon, you don't have to story to me," he said, trying to comfort me. "I know what you said is true. I know, too, that if I hadn't poked fun of your flour sack drawers you wouldn't have come out with it. I'm more to blame than you are. I started it.

"Lately I've overheard things myself that made me know Ma was a sick woman, but I never dreamed that I was held to blame. Now I know, and I'm glad I know."

"Reckon Grandma is going to die, Uncle Jule?"

"Course not," he said, reclaiming the reins and shaking his head to vanish the thought. "I talked to Dr. Miller just the other day and he told me Ma was in no immediate danger. Just the same, whatever's wrong with her, I'm responsible. I'm the villain of the piece. Seems I sentenced my pore old Ma to a life of misery for getting myself born." Uncle Jule's voice was calm, sober, deliberate, but the hurt came through just the same.

"Sounds like I done it on purpose. The Lord forgive me for layin' the burdens of life on an innocent child, but if I don't let off some of the steam churnin' in my guts, I may just may explode all over the place.

"Them women know Goddamn well that if it hadn't been for S.O.B. Julius turning up with the spondulix from shoveling horse manure six days a week at the O.K. Livery Stable in Melrose, Ma, Pa, Ethel, and you, too, would have had to make it on rabbit and beans this summer. It takes wherewithal to bring home lard, flour, coffee, molasses, and coal oil. As for Frank, he got a summer job all right—but we won't go into that."

I shriveled in humble humiliation. I knew, like a child knows far more than grownups think, that Mama met the RFD man at the mailbox every Wednesday only to come back empty-handed, biting her lower lip to hold back something, nervously twisting the hem of her waist apron into a ball. I knew all right. I knew that Daddy's dedication to books, especially the poetry kind, had somehow affected his ability to get and hold a job. But deep in my human self I knew, too, that I was like him. Even at seven, crowding eight, I loved books and rhymes, and I wanted to go to college, too.

While the spinning wheels of the buggy pursued a smooth road across a gentle, grassy stretch of cattle land, a melancholy silence fell between me and my beloved uncle, who ten and a half years earlier had been my age. I wanted to tell him not only that I loved him, but that his clean habits held a special place in my life. Sure, he chewed Brown Mule. All the men did. But Jule never spat the juice in the stinking spit-and-ash bucket by the stove. He didn't even lift a stove eye and spit in the fire well. Like the gentleman he was, he always went outside to get rid of his spit.

I wanted to tell him a lot, but a glance at his troubled face warned me that he was about to explode all over the place like he had said, so I kept still.

He did explode, but it wasn't too bad. It was just a "Goddamn," but he hollered it so loud that Blackie got scared and broke into a lope that lasted until we came to the signpost identifying "Monday's Wash," that ran only after a heavy rain, which meant almost never. Jule reined Blackie down and called her "Girl." He never could stay mad long.

The barely moving vehicle approached a dog town on the right, and a little brown prairie dog mounted the rim of his burrow and sassed us intruders with daring, impudent, barks. His message delivered, he audaciously wriggled his fat little tail and ducked into his hole.

"That's his way of thumbing his nose," Jule said, and we both laughed. The sun broke through a cloud of gloom and Blackie, steady, but still salty on the ribs, took the steep walls of the wash like a good horse should. Jule halted her on the opposite bank while he rolled a smoke and lighted up. He took a draw and then used the cigaret to point.

"See that sign over there on the post holding the three strand wire? It marks the boundary between Monday's Wash and Tom Irving's ranch, the T.I., only years ago some joker filled the initials in to read Tuesday's Ironing. That caught on, and even the township map shows Tuesday's Ironing next to Monday's Wash. Old Tom himself changed his brand to a flatiron."

"Really, Uncle Jule?" I had heard that story a dozen times, but I wanted to be friendly.

"Sure as shootin'" he emphasized, staring across the grassy, vast evenness of Tuesday's Ironing. "Mighty pretty! Mighty pretty!"

Seeing that Jule's eyes now were more blue than gray, I leaned on his shoulder and he kissed the top of my head. Although Blackie was ready to go, he wasn't. Not yet, anyhow. Taking off his stetson, he let the cool New Mexico breeze fan his sweaty, soft brown hair.

"I'd give my eyeteeth for it." He pointed to the windmill tower standing guard on rim of the spread. "Plenty of water, best grass on the plains, and easy fencin'. Tom's too damn old to handle it right anymore. Besides, that uppity woman of his wants to go back East to Kansas City where she still thinks she can sing in the opry. She calls cacklin' like a layin' hen singin'.'"

Once more he hungrily surveyed the cattle spread. Then he set his wide brim hat to dip a bit over his left eye, like real ranchers do, and the wheels began to turn. In a little bit a big square wooden box emerged on the tight rim of the prairie. It was the Ard schoolhouse.

Blackie was in good shape when we got there, but telltale salty streaks still showed on her ribs. Brother Bascomb, the balding, redfaced preacher who was hitching at the next post, looked her over, and biting his lower lip in suspicion said to Jule, "You been runnin' her?"

Acting like he didn't hear, Jule removed and reset his stetson. "Pretty day!" he said in greeting. The men shook hands and the preacher said, "Mighty pretty!" Just the same he shook his head, and looked Blackie over in doubt.

Then he went to help his family down from their double-seater. Each well scrubbed young'un took his daddy's hand and jumped to the hard, bare ground and began stomping ants. Their daddy had to use both hands, though, to provide safe descent for his frail, stoop-shouldered wife who had a faint mustache and who, according to the neighbors, took paregoric.

Other church-goers began driving up and hitching, but most stayed by their vehicles, waiting for the preacher to ring the bell after he had gone over his notes and Miz Bascomb had laid the song books out on the benches. Jule and a fellow he knew exchanged smokes, while I stood close to the buckboard, consciously aware that no matter what the preacher's young'uns did, a nice girl dressed for Sunday school didn't mess around with ant hills.

When the bell rang, Jule took me by the hand. "Hon, let's you and I keep what we talked about on the way over a secret just between us, and never, ever, mention it at home. Promise?"

"I promise."

We crossed our hearts, and then he straightened the wrinkles out of my dotted swiss dress and retied the blue ribbon sash. From his shirt pocket he produced a small white card bearing a gold cross and a quotation. "Ethel said you forgot it. I reckon you know your lesson." I nodded.

"I almost forgot," he said, digging into his change pocket, "Here's a penny for the collection and an extra one from Ma for the starving Armenians. Now be sure to bring home your new Sunday School card."

The two of us walked across the barren, dusty yard to the door of the Ard schoolhouse that was a Campbellite church on Sunday. But only I would go inside. Young single men didn't. During warm weather when the windows were open they listened to some of the singing and maybe heard a bit of the sermon, but usually they did some horse trading, played mumblety-peg or "match-me," and talked about girls.

When the final doxology was being sung the boys would hurry over and line up at the door to see if they could get to take some girl home. If a fellow didn't have any luck, he would shrug and say he would ride over to the Ginster place and see whether he could take Ima or Lena out. Ima and Lena Ginster were mythical sisters a fellow would say he was going with when "up against it" for female company. But Jule didn't have to date one of the Ginster girls, not at that time anyhow, because he had Opal. He was being true to her, too, so when the congregation filed out, he took me by the hand and led me toward our buckboard.

Suddenly, we came face to face with a plump, graying, sweet-faced woman wearing a black bombazine dress and men's shoes. Releasing my hand, Jule embraced the woman and wiped tears from her light blue eyes with his bandana. With the woman were two freckle-faced boys a little taller than I. Each politely shook hands with Jule, and then he beckoned to me. "Come, Leaf Marie, and meet your Aunt Noonie and your cousins."

Natively shy and utterly surprised, I just stood there. "Cat's got her tongue," Jule apologized, and Aunt Noonie broke the ice.

"Leaf Marie—what a pretty name!—you and Nim and Alf see who can run the fastest to the bobwar gate and back and the winner will get the stick of horehound I've got right here in my satchel."

It was only about fifty yards to the open, single strand gate, but the three of us ran so hard in the first spurt that we got winded and walked back. It didn't matter, because Nim was so far ahead he was sure to get the stick of candy anyway. But he knew what was expected of a little gentleman, so he took the horehound stick and broke it into three pieces, keeping the smallest for himself.

We newly-met cousins sucked on the brown, bittersweet treat, getting our fingers and lips all sticky. Aunt Noonie wiped our hands and faces on her handkerchief and said, "You all play for a few minutes while Jule and I talk."

By now I had my tongue back, and laughed and teased along with the boys, who could turn handsprings. I could, too, and better, but I said I couldn't because I didn't want to show my drawers—not only because of the printing on them but because nice little girls didn't.

Aunt Noonie and Uncle Jule spoke confidentially for a while and then called us to come. Jule helped the boys into their old buggy, and after another tearful embrace, he assisted Aunt Noonie to her seat. Then he unhitched the sorrel, gave her the reins, and everybody called, "You all come." The parting greeting as uttered by Aunt Noonie and Jule had a reason to sound hollow, for I had caught enough snatches of their conversation to know there was a wall between our two families.

I wasn't surprised then, when on the way home Jule said, "Hon, maybe we ought not to say anything about who we met today. Maybe you know why and maybe you don't."

"I know," I said. "Uncle Nimrod is in the pen and Grandma won't let us associate with his folks."

Jule was quiet a minute. Then he declared, "Aunt Noonie is a good Christian woman. She and the young'uns were visitin' her Pa over McAlister way, but she got up at daybreak to drive seventeen miles to get to church. And she's the only member of the family who didn't turn her back on Aunt Pet, but don't ask me about that."

I didn't but I was itching to, for I had overheard enough at home to know Aunt Pet, Grandpa's half sister, had gone crazy.

Jule spoke again. "Hon, I can see why Ma hasn't got no use for Pa's brother Nimrod. Rustlin' is against the law. He broke it and he got caught and sent up. But that's no excuse for snubbin' his innocent wife and children. It just ain't right."

I nodded in agreement. "What for makes Granny act like that, you reckon?"

"You'd have to understand how much it means to her to be 'quality'. Her Pa was a high monkey-monk back in East Texas, a senator or something like that. They had a big white house and Ma was brought up to believe the Ragsdales were cut off a finer bolt than the Bagbys. That's what Aunt Goldie claimed, anyway."

"Then why did she marry Grandpa?"

"Hon, honestly I don't know the answer. Maybe it was because—well, you know how sort of humped and spindlin' Ma's always been and Aunt Goldie—she's dead you know—said Pa was a mighty tall, handsome blacksmith, even if he was a Bagby.

"No, Siree," he went on, "I don't know what makes anybody get like they do. I just want peace. So maybe we better cross our hearts over a second secret, never to tell who we met at church. Ma is a sick woman."

On that memorable Sunday when I was going on eight, I once again crossed my heart. That heart was still crossed when many years later my beloved uncle was laid to rest at Rock of Ages next to his Ma and Pa with space left for Opal.

3

She returned the intimate, familial chapter to its niche in memory's file and continued to plod and remember, occasionally blotting a tear on the sleeve of her old fiesta blouse. Pretty soon she became aware that the dark undercoat of malpais seemed to be yielding its weird upchuckings to a more civilized terrain. What a relief!

Her shadow child reminded that she still had a few more walking hours of the day left, so she released her burden to take a breather. Looking about, she was surprised and delighted to see a rose-gray cloud actively beckoning from the earth-sky seam of the western horizon. This was a good omen. Tense and atremble she watched the shining cloud roll back a curtain and reveal a vast stage occupied by the massive shoulder of a great bowing rock that looked as if in some lost time, an even greater shoulder had nudged it out of the way to move on. This landmark was not new to her, of course. She knew it, knew what it stood for, and with consuming expectation she implored its good offices to reveal its companion pieces and establish bona fides of a cherished manifestation.

Holy Moses, it did!

The precisely truncated purple stumps of the four enchanted mesas beyond the rock placed themselves in scene. Two facing two, they stood out against the radiant morning sky in high geometric clarity. So far, so good. With a hand to her breast in taut expectancy, she watched a gauzy, opalescent vapor spread over the total sky range, only to float away on a sudden spray of wind leaving the stage utterly bare, but only for a second or so. In one ecstatic moment the scene was dominated by the map of her long, long sought goal. Then the picture dissolved into shimmering distance, magnificent shimmering distance. She knew the chain had not been broken. She must hurry.

With the packed and girded Two Grey Hills swinging from her resolute shoulders, she set forth again in the direction of her ultimate destination with hope asoar, for never before had the Fifth Mesa seemed so near.

After about half a mile, maybe less, she crossed a vega where alfalfa once had grown, and still showed up in spots, to a place where dilapidated old frame houses stood.

She wondered whether she should take shelter there. She had an innate disinclination for enclosed walls. Nevertheless, there had been times when this quirkness had been subjected to compromise and one more shouldn't matter. She headed for the largest building.

Releasing the burden from weary shoulders—it had been a rather tiring day—

she let the pack rest on the bottommost of three eroding, brick-based steps that led from the pot-holed, gravely street to the entrance of the old flat-faced, wooden hotel. What she needed most right now as a place where she could rest her bones and think things over. Espying a relatively clear space on an adjacent step, she modestly gathered her skirt so her knees would be properly draped, and bent to sit, only to straighten up. And mighty darn quick, too. The step was crawling with large, blood-red ants, and her last packet of bluing had been used up the time she had neglected to shake a boot out one morning, and a bare foot had encountered a dozing scorpion.

Being natively respectful of the territorial rights of fellow creatures, she and her burden removed to the far end of the tier, so the disciplined maneuvers of the little master builders, who were constructing a connoidal temple over an earth-clogged break in a riser, would not be interrupted.

Although this long-unused end of the row of steps was plagued by runners of wire grass, she knew how to handle it. You just had to find the terminus, jerk and wind. Naturally, a considerable amount of dust and rootage had to be blown and scraped off, but a clear sitting place was prepared in two shakes, and she was able to lower her weary body to an acceptable, if not luxurious, resting place on the second step, hinging her knees to allow her tired feet to occupy the first. Looking around she supposed this must have been a pretty lively place at one time. The barely legible, shot-up sign over the front door read: EMPIRE HOTEL & BAR.

She carefully tucked the folds of her plum-colored velveteen skirt beneath her muscular thighs so her knees could modestly swing aside to make room for the feet of anyone entering or leaving the hotel. There was, however, no evidence of any such activity. The only passerby was an astonished coyote, who apparently had expected to transact some rascally business in the vicinity of the hotel. Thwarted, he became a gray semicircle, and with his tail hanging down, disappeared into a thicket of rabbitbrush, as if going home mad.

Reading the western sky, she realized the final minutes of the day were ticking off. Poised like a red balloon on a seal's nose, the sun was ready to exit the ring. As one upon hearing the whistle of a train he is going to take feels a sudden reverence for his home, she felt a tightening of heart strings for the earth and sky. But she was able to mitigate the situation with the bright prospect that she and the stars would be separated for only one night. At least, she hoped so.

Arising, flipping grass chaff from her faded fiesta skirt, the only one she had at present, fussing a bit with her hair, she shouldered the Two Grey Hills and ascended the steps, pausing just beyond the threshold of the half-open door to let her eyes become accustomed to the dimness of the room. When a wooden counter stationed some eight feet from the dorrway identified itself, she approached. On its surface lay an open ledger, Bible-size, dust-laden and yellowed by time. She knew what the book was for, because she had seen guests sign while she waited in the lobby of the Antlers at Tucumcari for her father to show up. She looked about for a pen, but saw none. There really was no call for one, for the blue-bellied glass ink-well had suffered a long season of drought.

Balancing the packed and cinched Two Grey Hills on her head in the manner of a Mexican woman carrying a basket of chips, she used both hands to try to locate the stub of cedar pencil she kept in the elusive pockets of her velveteen fiesta skirt. In the search she emptied onto the counter a small comb, a dainty, celluloid-framed mirror that had come in a box of crackerjacks, a pillbox of talcum, a packet of needle and thread, a card of safety pins, a pocketknife, a jar of menthol, six matches held by a rubber band—just think, she had started out with a whole box—and a handkerchief knotted around two nickles and a copper. But no pencil.

Believing it to be gone for good, she was putting everything back in place when her fingers announced that the pencil had only been caught in ravelings and, indeed, was ready for action. The dust that couldn't be blown off the open register was wiped off with a sleeve.

In the arched backhand that had been analyzed at a Quay county fair as show-ing intelligence, imagination, and dedication to fair play—an interpretation that had played no small part in the patterning of her way of life—befitting registry was accomplished under the smiling approval of a fair-haired woman of exceptional beauty who stood against the wall back of a longer, higher counter.

NAME:	Leaf M. McIntosh
ADDRESS:	New Mexico, The World
OCCUPATION:	Pilgrim
PLANS:	Single Night's Lodging

"Yes," she assured herself as she restored her personal accoutrements to their habitat in the capacious pockets of her ample skirt, "It will just be for one night."

Turning away from the register in the self-confident manner of one in proper residence, she took a good look at the lobby that appeared to contain little except a huddle of broken-down pieces of furniture that looked as if they were waiting to be carted off and dumped in an arroyo.

Darkness was about to totally ghost the lobby of the Empire and its pathetic holdovers from a more prosperous era, so she retrieved her pack and wearing it over her shoulder like a sleeping young'un, she waved friendly-like and said, "Good even-ing to all. See you manana."

With a key to Room Five in her hand, arbitrarily chosen because five was her lucky number, she proceeded down the corridor aware without concern that little black seed eyes were peering from floor cracks.

Upon her discovery that Room Five and its key matched in number only—a closer relationship being obviated by an absence of lock—she blessed them both A lock by its nature connotative of restriction, she applauded its non-attendance Already feeling less cloistered, less nostalgic for her roof of stars, she humped the pack to clear the doorhead and entered.

The day-close dimness of the modest room lent an almost reverent liliness to a fragile, wrought iron bedstead. A tender climate of prior association made itself felt, and the delicate headframe and its junior counterpart at the foot of a dusty faded, cotton tick mattress metamorphosed into greater and lesser spiders. Memory tugged at her sleeve, begging to be heard. Why, of course, Grandma's old spider bed! She, herself, had been born on a spider bed, and she extended a friendly hand of recognition.

When the Caprock plain had been opened for settlement, claim seekers moved in by the hundreds. An enterprising eastern manufacturer had been quick to ship a whole boxcarful of white iron bedsteads of the spider design to a merchant at Mel rose, who gave credit against crops. Many of the dugout-dwelling homesteaders including the Bagbys, bought at least one. Theirs was for Grandma. Grandpa, too really, although he generally preferred to sleep on some old quilts, spread on corn shucks in the barn.

The eye of her mind saw a small, barefoot girl wearing a calico frock and flour sack drawers bouncing on Grandma's spider bed, building up to a window height that would provide a triumphant, although fleeting, view of the entire premises—the horse lot enclosed by bobwar-laced cedar posts, the shiplap lumber barn with the corrugated tin roof, the little privy with the hen house to match, and, most exciting of all, the face of the great, rotating daisy atop the skeletal windmill tower standing proud sentinel over the whole shootin' match.

The revisit to her childhood borned a feeling of sibness with Room Five. Working against darkness, she placed the gray-brown, zigzag pattern Navajo blanket, still thong-tied into a sausage-like satchel, across the flat top of a shadowy accessory near the foot of the bed. In the waning afterglow of sunset, she couldn't tell for sure, but she was ready to bet a copper cent it was a table converted from an empty wooden crate and a swatch of oil cloth, for inspite of the airs put on by the lobby, this had been a poor man's hotel. In the same context, she reckoned that without the gratuitous offices of the grocery store cracker box, the flour sack, and the Sears Roebuck catalogue, a lot of hard-up homesteaders would have been deprived of a lot of life's essentialities. And that's a Godalmighty fact. She could swear to it.

Although not particularly hungry, she knew she would have a hard time getting to sleep with an empty belly, so she got out the canteen, the drill bag of nuts, seeds, and Morman tea, and a tinfoil-covered rasher of jerky she had toted for Heaven knows how long, maybe too long. She put it back in the bag.

She ate little—a person likes to see what he is putting into his mouth—and then she put everything away, firmly cinching the leather straps. Several years ago she had learned a lesson about food preservation the hard way, when a blizzard had driven her to seek shelter in an abandoned schoolhouse near Ojo Caliente. That time she forgot to secure her food cache, and it was reduced to shells by little night visitors.

She still had her coat then, and when the blizzard let up, she buttoned up and departed the old schoolhouse without viaticum, in other words, unprovisionally. For two hungry months she scrounged along the right of way of the D & R.G.W. (Dangerous and Rapidly Growing Worse) tracks, finding almost nothing to eat. One day she sat down under a scrub cedar near the culvert where she had slept, seriously wondering whether she was going to make it any farther. Then fortune smiled. A Chili Line freight rumbled past, and a ragged, bearded hobo was sitting with his legs hanging out of an open boxcar door. He hi-signed and tossed out a big bag of goobers. That night she dined sumptuously on peanuts seasoned with wild asparagus and boiled in an old tomato can over a fire made from pieces of coal picked up along the Denver and Rio Grande Western tracks.

But that happened a long time ago. She sentenced the intrusive memory to go stand in the corner with its back to the class, and removing her boots, she placed them side-by-side on the edge of a pale satin rug laid across the floor by a shaft of mother-of-pearl moonlight slanting through the room's lone window. Then she modestly retired into the gloomy shadow of an unrecognizable piece of furniture where she shed her skirt and blouse. In drawers and camisole, she submitted her weary bones to the sagging alien couch.

The head and foot spiders nodded in polite recognition, displaying better manners than the musty old cornshuck-stuffed, cotton tick mattress that muttered audible complaint. Lying quietly on her side, trying not to arouse the husky grumbling and its concomitant dust, she cautiously unlidded the menthol jar, placing it near her face. Then she settled down for the night.

4

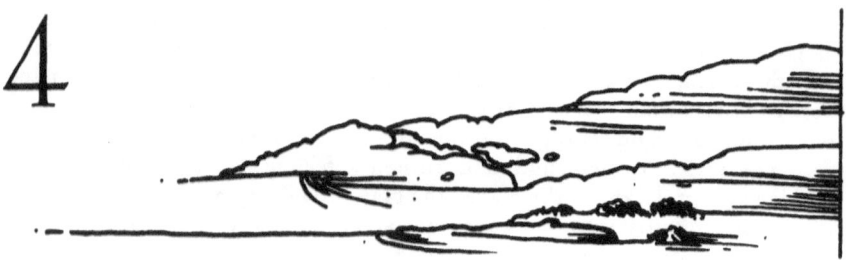

She must have slept well, for daylight walked in on the scene unexpectedly, hinting dereliction of duty, reminding her that she should have been well on the road by this time. She realized this, but for some reason she seemed unable to prod herself into action. Cradling her head on a fleshy pillow of arm, she surveyed the strange room, now unstrange.

Dehaunted by daylight, certain shadowy features of the room assumed clarity. The ghost that stood in a corner all night turned out to be a splay-footed pole pegged for hanging garments. The rectangular shadow on the wall over the bed proved to be a hauntingly memorable colored print, unframed, ragged at the edges, but of enduring pathos. She knew the picture well. It came when you sent in twelve Arbuckle coffee coupons plus ten cents postage and was entitled, "The Rescue." It showed a great, furry dog with a tired face innocent of fear, resting on a lonely, wind-swept shore of a raging sea from whose storm-tossed waves emerged a telltale, broken mast. Across the mastiff's paws lay a small girl in semiconscious sleep, her flaxed curls and blue-sashed dress drenched with salt spray.

Time turned the pages back and a tear came. A copy of the picture hung over her childhood cot for many years. Then, as now, her heart went out to all good and brave dogs, including her own Cojo, who was lame. His left front paw got chewed up by a bobcat when a puppy. Lopgaited, he always ran ahead, nosing mesquite and rabbitbrush to flush out anything that might menace her path. Then one day a pack of coyotes came by with a bitch in heat. Gone many years, Cojo's memory still lingered in a golden frame.

But a new day was at hand. It was time to close the door on the long ago and become acquainted with the is. Tightening the cap on the menthol jar, whose aroma of peppermint provided the only means of defense she had ever employed or needed, she reached for her skirt, inserting the aromatic container into a button-down pocket, inviting her conscious self to bear witness. Her memory, at least for day-to-day activities, didn't seem to be as good as it once was. Only a couple of months ago she had walked off, leaving the jar where she had camped some fifty yards off the old Camino Real. This caused her to have to backtrack for at least five miles.

It was a good thing that at that time the juniper had not released its infernal pollen, so her normal sense of smell was able to lead her back to the clump of snake-weed still flattened by the imprint of her blanket. Under the guardianship of the midmorning sun, the brave unlidded yellow jar was patiently awaiting recovery. But it was never as pungent again, even when stirred by a forefinger.

Sitting up in bed, she became aware of a lack of perversity on the part of the cornshucks. Apparently they had become resigned to her presence, or, on the other hand, maybe they were natively less sensitive to daylight. Anyway, it was good to be able to move without hearing complaint about being disturbed.

Habituated to matutinal routine, her fingers unbraided her hair for fixing up. In the combings she found a hair much lighter than the rest, really almost white. Wondering how it got there, she flicked it away. Still sitting on the bed, she separated the dark fall into three parts and rebraided, mindful to tightly feed in vagrant strands that had a habit of pulling loose and hanging about her face as the day wore on, especially if a wind came up, which it usually did.

When she lowered her coffee-colored feet in getting out of the bed, she got a surprise. The silent carpet of snuffy floor dust was cross-stitched by an exquisite network of little paths. Some of them had been left by harmless nightworkers like the chacho, but among them were the serrated trails of the centipede, the scorpion, and the cone nose bug. Apparently uninhibited by the aroma of peppermint, the crawlers had made a night of it. It seemed a shame to have to disarrange their artistic patterning—until she observed that their rounds included the vicinity of her squaw boots.

Quickly reaching for the right boot, she detected a suspicious movement inside. Still tweaked by the scorpion in her boot that time, she hurried the pair to the bedroom window, long innocent of glass, and gave them a good shaking. She had to laugh, though, when she flushed out a dozen or so wedge-winged, linty, miller moths that zigzagged in dazzled flight into nearby mesquite bushes. They were harmless, of course, but messy. Turning the soft uppers of her footwear back, she pounded the mill pollen out against the outside wall. She didn't cough once.

She stood at the window a few minutes inhaling the chiefest of a New Mexico triumverate—fresh air, frijolis and chilis. Today there was an added ingredient, a spiritual something giving sweet substance to her human self, whispering that in pursuit of her quest, she was about to penetrate the miraculous sphere of influence transcending the frontiers of human limitation.

She took her own good time dressing, having a bit of breakfast, straightening up the room, feeling deliciously aware that instead of Room Five confining her human soul as she had feared, it provided an easy atmosphere of privacy like a woman needs sometimes.

Then eager to hit the trail, she began to pack up. Something hidden in her bones spoke up, however, cautioning against being led by a hurrying hand, reminding that the way behind was strewn with inglorious monuments to incautious turns, and the way ahead could not be expected to be less venturesome. This time she was playing for keeps, and she must be patient and await further manifestation.

Stretching out on the old bed, she meditated upon the profound obligations of her mission. As she had done often before, she wondered why a simple country woman unendowed with exceptional talent or quality had been chosen for the magnificent errand? Perhaps the answer lay among other ponderables to be weighed on the Fifth Mesa. She hoped so.

After a bit of sudden sleep that couldn't have lasted more than five minutes, she elected to acquaint herself with outside surroundings, not knowing at what moment the gravitational pull of the loadstone would beam in her direction, sending her forth never to visit this place again.

Strolling about the deserted, weedy streets, she was saddened by a climate of exodus. Dilapidated old frame houses, dozens of them, structurally generic, akin in desuetude, stared with vacant eyes. It seemed as if some devastating epidemic had made the rounds—the epidemic of big company bankruptcy, she reckoned. She had visited ghost towns like this before where mines had played out, and not wishing to fall into the abyss of shadowness, she decided to return to the warmth of the hotel.

Then came a rustle of refreshing morning breeze, and on it the redolence of sage. Chamiza! Right there against a bobwar fence the gray-green shrub was shaking off winter's chains. Of all nature's growing things, she loved the chamiza best. Spreading her skirts at her beloved shrub's base, leaning her shoulders against its bowing branches, her mind went way back to the chamiza that grew along the snaky school house road.

Wiping the inevitable tear, the wayfarer recalled that one autumn several years ago, maybe as many as ten, she had visited that crooked old road, and was surprised that the chamiza was still there, some of the bushes five feet high, all dressed in yellow gold, permeating the empty prairie with a subtle redolence of spice. Her family home place, and the schoolhouse, of course, gone.

Memory having surfaced and spoken, she handed it its hat and waved it away. Recollections were predisposed to sidetrack the day's obligations, and they never settled a darn thing. Least of all a person's innards. Right now she had to cope with a touch of heartburn that seemed to crop up lately when least expected, and she wondered whether over the years she had developed an allergy to chamiza pollen, among other things.

She used to carry a little poke of soda scraped up at the Jemez Soda Dam for just such emergencies, and mixed with a cup of water, it did the trick. But that soda sack had been exhausted ages ago! Then she remembered hearing Grandma say that chewn young tumbleweeds were good for up-acid. Fortunately these juicy, green sprouts were at the right stage for usage, not mature enough to have stickers, yet far enough above ground to be free of grit. On her way back to the hotel, she stooped from time to time, pinching off young thistle tips, masticating them, swallowing the bland licquor and spitting the pulp. In a few minutes, she forgot all about the cardialgia.

She settled down again on the place on the steps she had cleared the evening before, this time with greater ease and self-confidence, again properly draping her skirt about her knees, having been brought up that way. Now being in residence, she could relax and enjoy the scenery.

She had an unlimited view of the splendid landscape—the immediate sheer rock escarpment diking into violet-tinted infinity, the back drop of purple mountains far, far to the west, and, even more soul-stirring, the gentle valley below. Embracing her hinged knees, looking down across the shining river-fed expanse, she reckoned that a silent, grassy valley on a spring morning was the most beautiful thing on earth—a proud confutation of all the ugliness and meanness in the world.

Abruptly, her eyes called attention to something she had not observed before. A great, barren scar incised the cedar-splotched wall of the right hand escarpment, exposing an unsightly, dead flow of impotent, oyster-colored ore in frozen issue from the gullet of a played-out mine, creating an ugly, downward path that extended onto the floor of the quiet, pristine valley, blaspheming the beauty of the whole vista. She was about to cry, so she got up and went inside.

16

The onward hand did not beckon that day, nor the next. Although she remained tense with expectation, the wait was not unrewarding. As days came and went, an atmosphere of pleasant, somnolent grace settled over the village, making it less bereft, and in time she became only peripherally aware of the ugly encroachment of worthless vein matter.

Besides, there was Lillian. Not only was Lillian endowed with extraordinary physical loveliness, she was blest with the gift of human understanding, providing a much needed warmth. Lillian's immaculate grooming, in contrast to her own shabbiness, rekindled an innate, although long-unspired, disposition toward keeping up appearances. She hated to admit it, but she felt icky-tacky all over in Lillian's presence. Furthermore, the face that looked back from her little celluloid pocket mirror with a pink angel on the frame was as ugly as homemade sin. Not only that, but, to put it mildly, her body didn't smell like a rose. She was glad Grandma could not see her grandchild now.

One morning, deciding it was high time she did something about it, she rummaged among personal trappings until she recovered a shriveled, utterly desiccated soapweed sponge. Moistening it at the mouth of the canteen, she placed it on the window sill to bloom, feeling the while, that the imminent ritual of purification not only would be more compatible with the Grail-like nature of her quest, but would honor the memory of Grandma as well.

Granny Bagby, nee Ragsdale, was persnickety about family cleanliness, as well as about moral nicety. Even after she took to her final bed, she would ask to be propped up on pillows so she could comb and plait her wispy gray hair, and she would ask Mama to place a pan of water, a washrag and a cake of castille on the up-ended goods box by the bed so she could make herself presentable. And she always modestly asked the family to leave the dugout when she had to use the "night glass."

The drought-conscious soapweed sponge on the window sill was disinclined to quicken, so she primed it with a second dose from the canteen. That did the trick.

She began to scrub, albeit somewhat brutally. When purified from scalp to sole, and clad in fresh camisole and drawers that had been washed and packed away embarrassingly long ago back at Horse Springs the time she was laid up a week with bilious cramps, she felt like a new woman.

The bath, like a bodily freshening does, perked up her mood. Casting her eyes Heavenward, she called, "Look Granny, I'm clean as a whistle!" But remembering that the whistles she had known often smelled of breath and spit, she sought a more refreshing figure of speech. The only other simile that came to mind was "clean as a hound's tooth," and knowing what dogs eat and drink—although they certainly were more selective than chickens—she decided to let the original stand.

Just the same, in further token to Grandma's penchant for proper grooming, she decided to work on certain outer garments that suffered from wear and tear. There wasn't anything she could do about the bald places on her old, purple velveteen fiesta outfit where the nap had worn down, especially in the vicinity of the armpits of the blouse. She could do something, though, about the sagging rows of silver braid that loosely surrounded the skirt. She had paid Ilfeld's $16.95 for the supposedly authentic squaw outfit to wear to fiesta many years ago, but the bridge was washed out by a flash flood the night before, and she didn't get to go. It was a good buy, though, and had lasted quite a few years. It just needed a little mending, that was all.

Without her glasses—they had been broken during a hailstorm a few miles east of Wagon Mound one spring—she had a devil of a time inserting the spit-twisted skein of thread through the reluctant eye of a needle. But right when she was about to give up, hitch was made and the loosened hammocks of tarnished braid were firmly reestablished.

Looking herself over, she had to admit that thanks to Grandma, partly anyhow, her personal appearance had now taken a turn for the better. She sure hoped Lillian would notice. In a further gesture of feminine enhancement, she got out her pillbox of talcum and whitened her face. Raking her teeth across her rough lips, she decided to soften and redden them up a bit with the rind of a prickly pear from her food bag. Then inspired to go whole hog, she loosened her plait of straight, dark hair, combing it out, and in ambitious mimicry arranging it into a crown on top of her head like her new friend, a lady of fashion, wore hers. She knew the hairdo wouldn't stay up long without the aid of hairpins, but she hoped it would stay in place until Lillian could see.

When she walked into the lobby erect and full bosomy, a pose she considered a bit saucy, she surmised Lillian looked approvingly. But her moment of high fashion collapsed when she opened the door to see what all the racket was. A vagrant tin can was careering down the street under a whiplash of wind that rocked the old door on its hinges. Before she could get it shut, the hairdo was down, flying every which way, confirming the wisdom of the old saw, "Never try to make powder and paint turn you into something you ain't."

The wind was just getting warmed up that day. Every morning for maybe a week, it came up stronger and stronger, working itself up to fever pitch by early afternoon, assaulting the creaking walls of the old Empire with all manner of debris and gravel. Nomadic tumbleweeds piled up against the enfeebled bobwar fence separating the hotel from a vacant neighbor, making a ramp that surplus, spinning brown spheres vaulted over like fleeing antelopes.

One dust-laden afternoon, the wind charged across the land with its tail over its back, pawing the dirt like an enraged bull. Awaiting evening when the fury should allay, she stayed in her tiny room, bracing against the building's sway, listening to the baleful hectoring of cottonwood branches as they lashed against the corrugated iron roof, creating the intimidating climate of a break-in. But the overwrought gale did not abate at day close as it had before, so she took the Two Grey Hills to the lobby where she could sleep, if sleep had the courage to come, near Lillian. Sleep was cautious in approach, but having someone to talk to made the hours seem less long, and after a while she found herself telling Lillian how it all had begun.

5

Although there had been previous moments, like in the hospital that time, when some supernatural influence stirred her soul, it was not until months, maybe even years later, certainly well after her recovery and the long, lonely walk back to the sheep camp, that the visionary had assumed an element of reality, assigning a mission to her life.

On that crystalline morning she was herding sheep on the altiplano, alone except for them and six pugnacious black goats to keep wolves away. With the sheep quietly agraze, she often became absorbed in meditation upon the many-faceted inequities of life on this planet. She questioned especially why life, as must be faced by conscious human beings, was such a far cry from what was taught by books, parents, even priests and preachers. If life was a struggle between God and the Devil, why did the Devil have the upperhand, especially regarding the violability of a woman's rights as a prideful human creature? What devious hand held the scales where fairness and discrimination were balanced?

A shot split the air and there was a death sound, the sob of a dying animal. A wounded doe struggled through the thicket to shudder and expire at her feet. No one claimed the body of the beautiful doe. A rumble of cart wheels echoed down the road and someone was singing. The briefly interrupted sheep continued to feed. Life beckoned that she take her aspen prod and go on as before, but she cried, "No! I must have an answer. For what purpose? For whose good was this harmless creature's life taken? I must have an answer."

It was then that the strange thing happened. Her eyes were drawn to the far horizon, beyond the sweep of the Rio Grande Valley, to where a great violet-tinted, tilted rock stood out in high perspective. Aware that the landmark was far out of her normal range of vision, she felt a strange prescience that it brought a message. She was sure of it when beyond the great, leaning rock, four purple guardian mesas, as precise as ink bottles, emerged two and two in perfect clarity and line. Impelled by a feeling of being reached out for, she gathered her skirts and hurried across a vega inhabited by wild buckwheat and purple vetch to a rounded boulder. Clambering to its top, she stared westward. She shielded her eyes with over-lapping palms, and watched a lilac-tinted mist billow high above the slanting rock and the four enchanted mesas. The amorphous vapor began assuming form, filling in, proving, smoothing, and in progressive steps shaping into a fifth mesa towering above the other four and the rock, creating a magnificent tableland so serene and soul-touching as to presuppose Truth.

The awesome majesty of the scene was so overwhelming that she closed her eyes. When she could look again, the total picture had diffused into honey-colored New Mexico sunshine. But she knew that she must seek and find this Fifth Mesa, for it held the key that would unlock the door to the logic of life, the sense of it all. There, if ever, would be revealed the ultimate reason for human suffering, poverty, hunger, heartbreak, humiliation, devaluation of dignity, and, above all, the frightening loneliness of a human soul for its home.

That's what she told Lillian, while the overconfident wind set out to confirm its status as conqueror of the world.

The storm petered out by morning, and the clean-swept new day was wrapt in radiant sunlight and bird song. Pushing back the folds of the Two Grey Hills, she sat up the better to see and hear through the front window. Her movements provoked a moment of guarded silence that without ceremony was broken by an unfamiliar bird call.

"Cheer-cheer-ratcheer-ratcheer." The leaves of the alamo outside the window fluttered and the strange call echoed from farther away, less audible, inaudible.

In the wake of the flight of the strange bird to its bright destination, an indecipherable, irreducible something made her know this was a simpatico hour. So impelling was the aura of prescience that she hurried to Room Five to assemble her belongings. She checked all the items in her skirt pockets to make sure nothing would be left behind this time. After straightening up the room a bit, she loaded her girded pack and bending to clear the doorhead, proceeded down the shaky old hallway for the last time. Turning in the key to Room Five, she waved farewell to the bosomy picture of Miss Russell that hung over the long-unused bar. Then, taking the far end of the steps going down, careful not to interfere with the colony of tiny fellow-creatures who were constructing a brand new pyramidal monument to whoever or whatever ants believe in, she departed Paradise, New Mexico—elevation 6756.

Surprisingly, the trail marker she picked up at the edge of town did not arrow downward into the lavendar-fawn valley as she expected but set forth upon an upslope involvement with the sheer Caprock escarpment that provided natural fortification for the vast, grassy plain lying above.

The labor and competence of design that had been put into the cobbled and cleated road to make it wide enough for wheels of a standard wagon or two horsemen abreast, implied that at one time the road had been extensively and purposely utilized. Eventually, abetted by more accomodating terrain, it became twice as big as itself for passing. Time and clime had had their say, of course. Potholes that could turn an ankle bedeviled the perilously positioned course, and occasionally she had to scramble across rock slides on hands and knees. Most plague-take-it of all were interruptions where some solifunctional terrace formed by creeping rocks and loose earth had eroded right down to the brink of eternity.

On the whole, she should not complain, though. Negotiating this road was a country stroll in comparison with what she had encountered the time she undertook an Indian trail up the wall of Frijoles Canyon. Besides, in all her travels she had never been favored by more enchanting vistas. From time to time she released the Two Grey Hills to rest her shoulders, and while fatigue slipped away and new vigor took up residence, she gazed in wonderment across the violet-tinted valley encircled by stern-visaged mountains preaching the morals of patriarchs.

"It is to the mountains one goes for wisdom, but in the valley one perceives the earth's soul," someone had said. She couldn't recall who. Swinging the Navajo blanket satchel-wise from her left shoulder for a change, she plodded ahead, thinking she would soon recall who said it, but she didn't. Actually, she didn't give it another thought.

Despite intervals of slow going, she made good time. The weather was just right, the advancing afternoon was mellow with good sunshine, and the air was pleasantly pervasive of cedar. As she tramped along, the propitious climate inspired speculation, and she pondered upon the ultimate end and purpose of the stubborn road that at various junctures could have climbed the rugged escarpment wall to pursue the smooth bordering plain. Why didn't it? An enticing element of mystery challenged her doughty will power, and she determined to see the road to the end. She didn't have to wait long.

The trail abruptly plunged headlong into a rock-strewn abyss. The road was gone. Unloading the Two Grey Hills, she wiped an astonished brow in disbelief. There simply had to be a reason, so she put on her thinking cap, the one with a feather on it. Her initial theory was that the road had been whacked off by some natural geological shift. Upon closer observation, however, she thought this not to be the case, not entirely, anyway. Unaffected surroundings indicated a one-shot deal. Embankment supports lay helter-skelter among unmutilated cedars. Undoubtedly some fiendish force had triggered a shot that drove iron rods, bolt collars, and all plumb through heavy timbers to stick out on the other side. Nature would have been less specific. It looked to her like a case of man pushing nature to too damn far. Be that as it may, hell sure had been caught on the wing.

Her probing eyes followed a path of destruction upcanyon to a sagging scaffold, an aged, rheumatic stork standing sentinel over a clutch of defeated old wooden shacks with caved-in roofs. On the side of largest was the bold aviso:
PARADISE 2 – DANGER! PELIGRO! – KEEP OUT! NO ENTRAR!
So this was Paradise 2, site of the mine disaster that set dogs howling over two counties and rattled windows as far as La Flor. Looking upon the mute wreckage, she stood in bone-tingling awe of nature. Although bountiful to man, it extracted a tribute. Man had a built-in obligation not to defile nature's magnificent pattern. Sometimes he went too far. Does nature have to strike back, she wondered, to keep total order on keel—the tragedy to some in reminder to the conscience of all?

She wished she had time to pause and weigh this, but right now she had to figure out some way to get out of this blownup canyon. With no visible exit, it looked as if she might have to backtrack to Paradise and leave the way she had entered. The thought was discouraging. In all her years of travel, she could count on the fingers of one hand the times she had been forced to turn back. There was something unprideful about turning back, like being called to account for something that had no validity or purpose. It seemed to her that the saddest of all human conditions was to labor in the shackles of a fruitless mission.

Her eye caught something moving about a third of the way up the wall of the canyon. A little higher, she saw it again and at better advantage. Fortune smiled. A wild burro was plodding a path leading up the canyon wall. She had to move fast, for the cedar studded sides of the escarpment already were sunless, and she could expect some tough going to where she could bisect the animal walk. Quickly readjusting her center of gravity for ascent, she proceeded with head and shoulders bowing with each step so in case of a fall she would not keel backwards, but would sink to her knees, automatically grasping for some rooted stabilizer, if nothing more than a tuft of grass. Fortunately, she had to scramble uphill for only about a quarter of a mile before she came to the animal path.

The trace was narrow, capricious, and rocky, but it was well defined by animal droppings, the impregnated deposits fertilizing minuscule, white-faced daisies whose song of spring made the climb less onerous. Just the same she breathed a heavy sigh of relief when she sensed the nearness of the altiplano, where she could walk upright with no fear of hurtling into eternity.

Another bit of luck, even more propitiously disposed, came with the discovery that the overhanging crust of the escarpment had been honed down into a gently elevating path. This, indeed, was a break, obviating the tricky acrobatics of vaulting the canyon's visor with the assistance of a pliant sapling, a feat often necessitated in her travels and invariably provocative of a backache.

The final rung of the ladder was accomplished with ease, and lo and behold she stood tall on the rim of a vast, horizontal plain of lion-colored grass! Resting a hand on the genial shoulder of a veteran boulder guarding the point of descent, she thanked the Source of Things, all things both great and small, for quickening her feet to safety.

Unharnessing the Two Grey Hills, she placed it across the accommodating surface of the formless old rock. Burden free, she relaxed body muscles, arching her back and twisting her shoulders from side to side. Inhaling the clean, high plains air, and feeling quite fit, she surveyed the vast, even llano, and then took a good look at the solitary boulder resting on the canyon's edge. It was not much of a rock, as rocks go. It was not big, nor was it a pillar of strength. Its sole distinguishing attribute, aside from a strategic location, was a smooth, wind-varnished side vulnerable to written word and etched symbol.

In the fading sunlight, she ran her fingers over the smooth page of the ancient tablet where inscriptions and petroglyphs spoke messages in stone. Using a nugget of charcoal from an earlier visitor's campfire, she was able to limn in and distinguish certain aboriginal petroglyphs—the undulating path of the going-snake, the looped rings of eternal life, and Zia, the symbol of the sun. Beneath them was the barely discernible outline of a rather large bird with wings spread in preparation for flight. It was the sacred figure of the thunderbird, the supernatural eagle, spirit of thunder and lightning, commander of the sky, and, along with Zia, the signature of New Mexico's Indian heritage. But it was a strange thunderbird that emerged from energetic wipings and blowings. Its neck feathers were scales, and it had the head, the face, and the tongue of a serpent. Now, below the sacred bird, the faint tracings of another form of life began to emerge. She quickly limned in the lean body of a coyote. There was a feather in its mouth! She stood atremble, touched by a deep, inward feeling that the primitive portrayal of the ancient conflict between earth and sky was not meant for her eyes. With a handful of sand she erased the drawing, leaving to time what belonged to time.

On the opposite side of the rock, off-face from the withering west wind and leaping across more recent history was the "Paso Por Aqui" guest list and trademark of the Conquistadores. Reading down, she observed that one A. de C.G. passed by here mes Avril ano 1540. The initials rang a bell, a bell that kept on tinkling while she rested with her back to the rock, chomping jojoba nuts, sipping just enough water to make them go down.

Memory's tinkle faded with the daylight, but wouldn't give up. Right when she expected it to retire beyond recall, it hit a responsive key and opened a book, Stories of the Conquistadores. Miss C. de Baca, her sixth grade teacher had loaned it to her. One of the tales was about an ill-starred explorer named Alfredo de Casa Grande.

What were his thoughts upon this spot so long ago? Did he dream of returning to his home in sunny Spain covered with glory, laden with gold, another man's gold? Or had he drawn his lonely track to this remote land seeking something more precious than a handful of yellow dust? Had he more than three centuries ago entreated these same stars for direction to a mysterious horizon where he would find what the world had lost? Who could say what his impassioned gray eyes beheld on that last day of his journey as he lay dying of thirst on a Kansas plain? Was it a joyous vision wondrous to behold?

Drowsiness took possession and her eyelids seemed to be trying to close over door knobs. Loosening the cap on the menthol jar, bidding the stars "Goodnight," she wrapped up head and ears in the warm folds of the faithful Two Grey Hills. It was quite chilly now.

When she awoke, the ultramarine sky was without a trace of cloud, and the morning air was of such translucence that it seemed not to be there at all. The exact hypotenuse of Leaning Rock bisected the prairie's tight tim, and a little to the left, in splendid color and form, stood the four enchanted mesas.

6

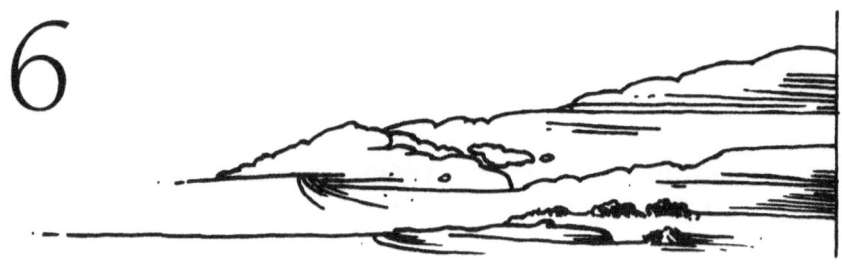

Her eager eyes did not have to explore for the Fifth Mesa. The exquisitely truncated lilac-and-pearl monument, created by nature according to statable mathematical precision, proclaimed its presence in high clarity for all the world to stand still and know. Tears filled her eyes, but the effulgence of the rising sun erased them, and the cause for their brimming.

The sun's rays had not yet moderated the pre-day chill when she heard the chatter of voices below the prairie's rim. Drawing the Two Grey Hills about her shivering frame, she stepped to the edge of the escarpment to acknowledge the matutinal greetings of a flock of muttering, stiletto-beaked pinon jays, who were inviting her to share their find.

She went down to a clutch of scrub pinones rooted in the off-sweep of upland soil, and joined the chattering, sky-tailored flock, scratching along with them for seasoned brown-shelled nuts containing the vanilla-colored goodness that provided health and well-being for all. With a lapful, she trudged back up to her site of temporary residence. Sitting with her back against the guardian boulder, she tossed selected nuts several at a time into the right side of her mouth where they were cracked by her teeth and husked by her tongue. The good meat was consumed simultaneously with blow-offs of chaff from the opposing corner of her mouth in a continual, facile process as amusing as it was induplicable to the uninitiated.

With breakfast taken care of, and quite a tasty one it was, she sighted the sun, which reminded that she should hit the road. While assembling her belongings, she carelessly stepped on her little pocket mirror with the celluloid frame, forever ending its reflective properties, and according to Grandma's augurings, letting herself in for seven years of bad luck. The incident caused only mild concern, however, just a fleeting twinge of sentiment. Daddy had found it in a box of crackerjacks and had given it to Mama, who was blond and pretty. Somewhere along the line it passed from mother to daughter. For her own part she saw nothing in the mirror worth looking at anymore. It was just one more thing to drag along, like something that for family reasons you would never deliberately discard when you moved, say a photograph of a second cousin you had never seen, yet, if it met with unpremediated mishap, it would never be missed.

With the toe of her boot, she maneuvered the slivers of glass under the edge of the boulder where nobody would step on them, opinioning that next to the tail of a cat, the most vulnerable thing in the world to the sole of a human foot, was a piece of glass. Then, using a sharp-edged stone as a stylus, she properly recorded her visit: "Paso Por Aqui, L.M.McI. Date (?) A.D."

With the Two Grey Hills firmly set on her back, she sighted far, far down the visual progression of the west-going trail. Through the transparent veil of morning, she could make out irregular heaps of far-off sad mountains that had the look of graves of prehistoric mammoths that had faltered and fallen while fleeing destiny. It was likely the trail would circumvent them. She hoped so anyway.

The air was cool and bracing. She stepped off the miles in rhythmic, measured tread. It was a good road, straight and relatively free of geological and vegetal impedimenta, and moreover, it was favored with an atmosphere of friendliness. Regal mullein stalks held their spikes at rigid attention as she passed, dainty, tomato-colored faces of globe mallow smiled back at her, and purple-eyed buffalo peas fluttered gray velvet aprons in salutation.

She made exceptionally good time, gaining steadily upon the distant barrier of blue mountains, and around midmorning was further inspired by a sound of good omen. Releasing the burden from her shoulder, porching her brow with a hand, her eyes were able to confirm what her ears had heard. Overhead, high above the range of the hunter's gun, a V of honking geese plowed the sky. How wisely they ride above extinction, she thought.

Not so fortunate were the passenger pigeons, whose irridescent neck feathers and ruby-colored breasts made them, according to her grandfather, the most beautiful of all American birds. He told how when he was a lad flights of passenger pigeons would blot out the sun. Now they were extinct. The stately whooping crane was rarely seen, and the hoop billed curlew was disappearing. The few buffalo left were in captivity, and the deer and the antelope were thinning out. Time was running out for the timber wolf, the coyote, the javalina, and the jackrabbit. Even the urban societies of prairie dogs were doomed. Fraught with an overwhelming sadness, she wondered what men and their lethal weapons would say to each other when they had finished their game? Would they turn upon each other? Would the world ever regain what it has lost? The only response was the eerily human cry of the wild goose.

The trail remained straight and easy for about an hour, giving her freedom of mind to ramble through musty old halls of memory. In their young days, she and Cousin Cooter, although he was several years older, shared a mutual aversion to the drudgery of broom-corn pulling. It was so messy. During harvest time, to make the rows less long, the two of them always managed to pull side-by-side, and would sing, recite, or even stomp any old thing that came to mind.

Reliving that bittersweet interlude, making sure no one was observing such nonsense, she lifted her skirts for stomping and declaimed:

Oooh! The hawk shot the buzzard
And the buzzard, shot the crow.
Ramble around the cane brakes
Shoot the buffalo!

Catching her breath, she then intoned an old favorite, The Preacher and the Bear, about a preacher who went huntin' on Sunday, strictly against church rules, and was treed by a bear. The high volume prayer at the end, "Oh, Lawd if you can't hep me, for God's sake don't hep that bear!" exhausted her vocal strength, so she opted for something less demanding. While wiping away the tears welling up from

"Over the Hill to the Poorhouse," she stumbled and went to her knees.

The reason her feet had let her down was because she had let them down. While she and Cooter were pulling broomcorn and carrying on, her unadvised feet followed the trail to an abrupt dead end. Unbelievably, she found herself standing on the shore of an ominous sea of sand.

The situation was puzzling, because there was no trace of a warning sign. The encroachment of the sand dune had apparently begun subsequent to the trail's loss of commerce. Observing the great stretch of intrusive sand, she opined that in five years, ten years, one hundred years or maybe a thousand or more, its course would alter. But Hell's Bells, her problem was immediate!

Being thoroughly seasoned to the vagaries of her native land, she realized how ticklish her problem was. While everything looked as friendly as a basket of chips right now, this was not the season of passive calm. At the fiendish whim of an equinoctial gale, the peaceful, sculptured waves at her feet could surge into a suffocating torrent, darkening the sun, parching the tongue, and even creating mental inbalance. That, of course, was on the negative side. On the positive side, at the moment, a northerly breeze pegged the temperature at a comfortable level, and away out yonder she could see a grove of trees, shrubs or something along a lake, so she figured the dune might not be very wide. Never one to shilly shally, not for long anyway, she opted to proceed.

Releasing her pack, she removed and tested the water canteen. It was more than half, and possibly three quarters full. That was good. Next she snugged and and folded the uppers of her goatskin boots about her ankles, firmly cinching the leather laces around the silver conches to keep the sand out. Then, using the selvage thread from a yucca leaf, she fashioned two wild gourd leaves into a sun visor. Arranging her pack to swing from her left shoulder in the manner of a child's school satchel, and looking around carefully to see if she had left anything out, she crossed her fingers for luck, and turning toward the west, set out across the sand.

At first sandburs grabbed the hem of her skirt and scratched her ankles, but soon they, the wild gourds, and all vegetation except an occasional yucca, disappeared. All went well enough until midafternoon, when the gentle, northerly breeze expired. The sun immediately stoked its furnace, drops of sweat oozed down her boney bare legs, and her bunions, especially the large one on her right big toe, ached from heatswell. The gourd leaf sun shade went as limp as Granny's dishrag, and the device had to be discarded. Her unshielded eyes then began to itch and exude salty tears, which, along with the drip of an involuntary sneeze, she wiped off on a sleeve.

While these little annoyances were irritating, they could not be classified as distressing, not yet anyway, and were by no means outside experience of one brought up on a dryland farm. A flabbergasting thing, though, was the sudden appearance of a field of tame vegetation alien to a barren region.

Wiping her face with the hem of her skirt, and shielding her eyes with crossed palms, she surveyed a roughly twenty acre plot of stunted, burlap-colored stalks, graphic and still as a harvest painting. It was unbelievable that anything at all, except maybe some breed of cacti, should grow in this isolated silicic area. Just the same, many of the stalks were emerging into feeble tassel. More baffling was that the east-west rows were laid out in precise agricultural conformity, yet there was no shred of evidence that man or machine had ever been there.

She put on her thinking cap, the canvas one with the air vents. At her starting point, she had seen trees and a lake ahead. But the trail had come to an end at a lower level than the dune itself. Hence, the diabolical mirrors of the desert had projected this minuscule straw island in a sea of sand, as a grove of trees bordering a lake. She had simply been tooken by nature again. It was as simple, or complex, as that.

Screwing up her courage that had begun to flap, she followed the edge of the outlandish grain field, wondering whether it, too, was out of the devil's bag of tricks. But the bonafides of the strange sorghumy-looking little field soon were established, albeit in an inhospitable manner. She stumbled over something hard and sharp and fell flat, Two Grey Hills and all.

After pulling her disheveled self together, she took a looksee at what the Sam Hill she had tripped over. It was the largest of what appeared to be disjoined pieces of a sizeable, old flat rock. When she discovered some sort of lettering on the crumbling fragments of sand-scoured stone, curiosity took over.

Fitting the pieces this way and that, she finally determined a date as 188?,— probably 1885. With that start, she was able to figure out AGRI. Then AGRICUL-TURAL fell into place, followed by EX. . . . . ., which naturally presented itself as a second adjective, EXPERIMENTAL, which presaged the noun STATION, except it didn't fit. But PROJECT did. So far so good. But not good enough. Two remaining words would tell the tale. She finally doped out that the first word, a five letter one, began with SU, and its companion, also of five letters, began with DU.

She went up and down the alphabet trying to make sense of the two reluctant words, but with no luck. Finally, a favorite subject, "geography" raised its hand asking to be heard. She took SU around the world and suddenly the pieces fell into place. "Eureka!" she cried across the desert silence. This indomitable, deserted, old field had been planted as an experiment with SUDAN DURRA, which has been able to survive North African aridity since the beginning of time. If she had not been so dumb she would have realized after the first sneeze that she had happened on the pilot crop of plain old feterita, the bane of her youthful existence. She wished she had a dime for every bundle of the commercially successful but personally detested result of this experiment she had toted, all itchy-eyed, to feed the cows.

"Well," she philosophized as she reared for journey, "Yesterday and today have known each other longer than you think."

Sighting her shadow, and figuring the day still had three, maybe four hours yet to go, she squared her shoulders and set out across the shoreless infinitude of sand. Actually, the going was less strenuous than she had feared. The way was free of obstacles, the sun seemed strangely less hot, and, of course, all traces of nasal or optical irritation soon cleared up. Aware that desert nights often were quite light, she toyed with the idea that she might pause in a couple of hours or so to rest and fix a bite to eat, and then tramp onward for a spell by starshine before she made camp.

The storm struck from behind. She turned quickly and faced the blast in dis-belief. A cloud of dust toiling high into the Heavens dimmed the sun. She had to act fast. Quickly, she untied the pack, using the romals to tie the canteen and the bag of personal possessions about her waist. Then, wrapping up head and ears in the Two Grey Hills, she fell to the earth.

Hour after hour, day after day, night after night, she lay in lethargic befuddle-ment curled up like a grub on an uneasy bed of shifting sands. Sometimes, parti-cularly at night, the gale would weary, and she would peek between the folds of the Two Grey Hills, hoping to see some of her friends, the stars, but they, too, were under cover. Later on, there came daytime lulls, and looking up she could see clouds of snuff-colored dust billowing high into the Heavens, while a tired sun peered down through a copper veil. Day and night became a series of revolving mirrors, for how long, she did not know.

Came a morning clear and still. Divesting the ill-smelling blanket, she looked out upon an endless, gently-waved sandscape as innocent as a dozing lamb. But how will it be at noon, she wondered, when the hungry wolf with his empty stomach dragging on the sand creeps up on the fold? She had known mornings like this, when the sky had a look of steel and the emerging sun seemed to be trying to shine through a metal mesh, and she was apprehensive, uneasy in her bones. Just the same, she would muddle through, somehow. At least she had a good record for survival of crises—so far, anyhow.

She knew she had not eaten for an x-length of time, and that she should be hungry, but uncertainty over the weather dulled the edge of any appetite for food, and that was not good. But when she espied the canteen, her mouth whindled like a thirsty babe craving a bottle. She lifted the flask, but dared not drink. It was much too light.

The depletion of her water supply put an ominous complexion on matters. As frustrating as the scarcity of water, was the solemn evaporative evidence that she had lain half-buried in the sand longer than she had supposed. Much longer. A lot of time had been lost. She set forth at once on a westward course as unchartered as on that first day on earth.

When the morning was about three quarters old, the sun rolled up the metal curtain and stoked its fires for some timely baking. Heat devils shimmied on the horizon and droplets of sweat coursed down her forehead and nose, spilling across her lips, leaving a taste of brine.

Around twelve by shadow contraction, she began to feel peculiar. Involuntarily raking her tongue back and forth across her lips, she became aware of a labial numbness. Her normally thin lips were puffed far beyond their natural boundaries. Instead of being alarmed, she found the anomaly rather amusing, imagining that she must look very, very funny. Furthermore, a pervasive sense of euphoria invited pert bouancy, jest, laughter, and even an indelicacy of thought and gesture. Her native self, ever dedicated to stubborn moral values, took a dim view of such obliquities of refinement, but was forced to stand aside and watch. Even more shocking than the lapsus moralis itself was the accompanying intimation that these digressions represented a natural and spontaneous part of life. But that was taking things too far away from her inherent sense of moral discipline. She realized though that it really didn't matter. All was only a dream anyhow.

Consciousness came and went over an indefinite space in time, each interval of awareness becoming more lucid and of longer duration. After a while, she found herself struggling to move her head away from the sun's stare into the spotty shade of a panicle of yucca. On the next round she knew she had cleared the sand because the grassy earth underneath the blanket was firm and comforting.

She had not been aware that she had fallen asleep again until she was awakened by ants crawling on her tongue. Sitting up quickly, seizing a handful of velveteen skirt, she used the soft nap to clear the ants from her protruding tongue. The lingual massage induced a vinegary formic secretion, making her gag. That was good. The nausea reactivated sluggish salivary glands, and she was able to coerce her bloated tongue back into its proper habitat. It still seemed too big for her mouth, though, and about to pop out.

Lightheaded, she lay back down. Some time later she was stirred from a deep, narcotic sleep by an exploding thunder clap. She sat up quickly, too quickly. Again she had to lie back down, but this time sleep stood off and watched, while she lingered in semiconscious adjustment to her surroundings, which, in a hazy way, appeared timely and kind. She was presently aware of the bestowal of a bounty that she could taste, hear, and feel on her scalp.

Sitting up without dizziness, she looked upon a scene of fantastic charm. A nearby crystal pool mirrored tendrils of overhanging foliage. Long-necked white birds stooped to drink, then, with outspread wings, flew into the hyacinthine distance. By degrees, the exotic scene surrendered its legendic aura, progressively assuming an atmosphere of conscious human experience. A pair of doves were drinking from a nearby buffalo wallow that brimmed with an evanescing, icy froth.

7

With clear eyes she saw that the new, blue sky had been washed and hung out to dry in the sun. The earth's fever had gone down and nature's rewards lay everywhere—in awakening blades of grass, in the virile, antiseptic breath of the creosote bush, in the tumid green girth of the hedgehog cactus, in the aromatic utterance of sage, and in the cool cling of her garments. A homey, wet-lamb smell pervaded the spread blanket where she sat. It had rained! Glory Hallelujah, it had rained!

Her fingers sought some curious knots on the back of her head. She could feel them, and they were sore. Her shoulders and back felt as if they had been beaten. Blue-black splotches showed on her thighs and on the backs of her legs. She had a good laugh on herself, for it had done more than just rain. She sure must have been dead to the world to have slept through such a hailstorm. When she rolled the Indian blanket up, she had another good chuckle on herself. She sure must have been minus her marbles when she spread her bed on an ant hill.

She set forth on a trackless, westerly course across a stretch of purple-sickled gramma so friendly she was tempted to stoop and stroke it. But her back advised that she forget it, there being a question whether a bend could unbend. Consciously stiffening her lagging frame, she kept on going but after a little bit she began to stagger. Then it dawned on her that she had neglected to eat before setting out. Actually, she couldn't recall when she had eaten last.

She saw green garden nearby, and crossing her fingers against the chance that she was being tooken by a mirage, she hurried, empty canteen in hand, to a small oasis sprung from recent hail melt. Quietly slipping past erect sentinels of woolly-based mullein stalks guarding the rim of the sudden pond where a wrinkled old buffalo wallow had been and would be again, she knelt to lap from a cupped palm, respectfully muffling the tongue-dips when she observed a pair of wild ducks sitting in intimate silence no more than twelve feet away. When she and canteen were replenished, they slipped away so softly, the ducks never knew.

Already having an eye on a patch of star tulips and wild onions growing near the banks of the water hole, she tugged at them, and as if in anticipation of her need they came right up. She hurried back to her waiting burden and sat cross-legged on the good-smelling grass with her thighs decently draped by the dismally wrinkled gores of her skirt. There she ate heartily of the roots and bulbs, wondering, the while, just how much traveling time had been lost. Her built-in body calendar indicated it was quite a lot. That wasn't good. Her mission simply had to be completed by the time cold weather set in, because she no longer had a coat. It has been burned up the time she had to flail her way out of a brush fire near El Cabezon. As for the wool sweater that had tided her over during cold spells, she hadn't the slightest notion what had become of it. One day when she packed up to leave a wind erosion cave where she had remained wrapped up in the Navajo blanket until the temperature went up, the sweater wasn't there. It was a shame because it was an expensive sweater, one of Ilfeld's best, $7.95 marked down from $10. But it was gone, and there was no use getting worked up over it.

She now felt rested, well-fed and quite fit—"fit as a fiddle," one might say, the traditional connotation being that violins were never unwell. Her own observation, although limited to square dance music, was that some of them sounded pretty sick. She really shouldn't pass judgment, though. Her knowledge of musical instruments was sketchy, being limited to the pump organ, the mouth harp, and the musical saw. And, of course, the eloquently pitched harp of the wind—the harp now playing sweetly, softly while she moved ahead, pausing only to reconnoiter for a trail marker. On that damnable arenose exploit, she and the trail had become separated, but she had the sneaky feeling they were within hailing range, and she felt that by continuing west their ways eventually would converge.

The southwest wind was breathing just heavy enough to keep the temperature in the seventies, confirming what the red rosettes on the limbs of the cholla were trying to tell. It was late June or early July, later than she had supposed, but not without promise. Aside from some oveny afternoons, she could expect three months of good walking weather.

For quite a spell, maybe as long as three weeks, she traversed a carpet of good grass. The weather was fine, summer showers kept the termperatures comfortable, and edible bulbs and grasses grew in abundance. Then one day the lush plain began to relinquish its claim to prosperity. The good grasses thinned out, yielding to runty sage and nicotine-stained hillocks of turpentine weeds that had a curiously oxidized look, as if instead of growing from the earth, they had been sloughed off as mine tailings. In the face of pathetic stretches of such useless, impoverished soil, her erstwhile bounce and spirit flagged. Land had to be mighty sorry for the turpentine weed to take over. Nothing would eat it. Not even a goat.

Eventually the rusty-looking desert weeds, the scraggly sage and rabbitbrush phased into equally uninspiring ringworm-like circles of drab round grass. For miles and miles she tramped the monotonous, unvarying plain, feeling environmentally trapped like a caged squirrel on a treadmill. To check the unhealthful symptoms of mental drag, she placed a thumb across a wrist and began counting heart beats, figuring that between sixty and seventy would roughtly clock a minute, or sixty steps closer to her lost trail.

For some unaccountable reason, thoughts of Columbus soon replaced the senseless heartbeat exercise. Plodding along, she understood how C.C., like any other pioneer, must have been plagued by nowherenessas, as day after day he sailed westward, ever westward, into a lonely infinitude. Then, on one gloriously auspicious dawn, there shone a light on a distant shore. Pretty soon she, too, became revivified in spirit when she saw a dark seam creasing prairie east to west. Like a horse headed for home, she broke into a trot.

As if the trail had been expecting her and had left the latch open, a welcoming boulder awaited at the intersection point with the initials CPT neatly blazed on its smooth surface.

Even though this section of the Cross Plains Trail long had lain unused, and its furrows were overgrown with wild gourds and quitch grass, the doughty old road was vibrant in spirit. Recent rain had fallen and the bordering ginger-green grasses lay smooth as a well-kept lawn presenting an atmosphere of neighborliness. In this context she saw, or thought she could see in the distance ahead a flock of neat, white sheep randomly at graze on the grassy sward.

But when she neared, and the sheep remained frozen, her disappointment primed a tear. What she had mistaken for sheep were rounded, gray-white boulders strewn over a grassy vega. Her imagination suggested that the plump, idle stones could have been left over from some recreational activity of prehistoric giants. Reversing the lens of her mind, she watched from a sideline while great, slope-shouldered, hairy adversaries swung heavy, gnarled clubs. But only for a moment. It was so ridiculous. She hoped the ghost of Dr. Baugh of La Flor College wasn't tuned in, or she would get a lecture on "morainic push."

Adjusting frame of mind and burden, she conscientiously pursued the favorably disposed trail. In a way they were old friends, for at various times during her pilgrimage, she had traveled other sections of the CPT. Hankering for small talk, she spoke about that, relating, as well, some of her experiences of fellow-trails—Pecos, Blue Water, Coronado, Old Santa Fe, and of course, El Camino Real, the main trade route between Chihuahua and Santa Fe, with its unique Bench of the Burros on La Bajada. There the laden donkeys, into whom nature had invested more intelligence than in their masters, simply sat down at the hair-raising bench and refused to budge.

She recalled that some of the trails she had followed had been quite spectacular, like the old one traversing the escarpment at Ragland, but for relaxing charm, and she meant every word of it, she would take the Cross Plains any old time.

She and the trail quietly went on and on, and the first thing she knew, the old road marched right up to an abrupt drop-off without so much as a "Watch Your Step!" Her first thought was that the trail had given up the ghost and gone over. But upon studying the situation, she learned it had merely digressed to the rim of the escarpment to reward a tired traveler with a change of view, as a proper trail should. And what a view it was!

In breathless wonder she looked down upon and out across a magnificent still life, a masterpiece in color and form. From the floor of the violet and henna valley arose an exquisitely turned red-brown olla. Not far from the urn stood a precisely-contoured tinaja, the capped, sandstone water jug graphically described by exploring Spaniards. In background relief, a diminishing tracery of limestone diking extended irregularly into shimmering infinity. Suddenly, an aura of familiarity permeated the splendid vista.

"El Puerco!" she cried.

Employing a bit of sleight of mind, she found herself looking upon this scene from the opposing rim of the canyon. She was standing over there by the El Puerco sign, tossing pinon nuts into her mouth and looking where the arrow pointed. A person really didn't need much imagination to make out the form of a dozing pig, snout, ears, and all—even a tail if you looked close enough. The olla was his passive body, the tinaja his trough, the dike his sty. Thinking back, she figured it must have been around four years ago that she had pitched camp for three days over there at Puerco Point to gather pinon nuts.

She stood in a curious atmosphere of mixed concept, wondering which of the valley's two faces was the true one? Was it the artistic still life in pottery or was it the pig sty? Or was there yet another face projecting neither? Her bemused thoughts sought to bring into comprehension, the strange patterning of nature's behaviorism, the kaleidoscopic deceptions of perspective, the trickery of mirage, the elusive enigma of Truth, the many, many faces alike only in the dark. But her process of reasoning was weak, and it was just as well that the sight of a horned sidewinder muscling his way over a nearby rock established immediateness.

Giving wide berth to the rattler, she set forth on the continuing trail that oddly assumed a scalloped pattern, curving inward toward the brink of the escarpment at spaced intervals, much in the cautious manner of a cat on a roof checking for the least formidable avenue of descent.

In about an hour or so she stopped cold. A more inhospitable descent could scarcely be imagined. Why, that downward slope was nothing more than a dump of treacherous red-black volcanic puke. Still, she had to take into consideration that the trail had been in business for some two hundred years, so there must be more to it than met the cursory eye.

Upon careful study of the hodge-podge of unsightly rocks, she was able to perceive a narrow, beaten path treading downward through a lava flow that had cooled for thousands of years but still looked too hot to touch. Knowing that this tricky path had been gouged out for a purpose, her agile hands had begun cinching the ties of her boots for rugged descent before her slower mind caught on. Even then she wasn't sure she was doing the right thing, but she went along anyhow.

The only good thing she could say about the crazy path was that it was free of nettle, barb, and fishhook. It was plagued, however, by sharp cinders that not only were inhospitable to her feet but were devastating to her only pair of footwear. At this critical stage of her pilgrimage, she dared not take a chance. Her feet could recover—they always had—but her boots did not possess self-healing properties. Off they came, and she wore them string-tied around her neck. The cruel rocks tormented the soles of her bare feet, bringing blood, but she kept on going.

In a little bit, something she had been hoping for began to shape up. Disengaging the lava flow, the declivitous path arrowed across a stretch of mossy, soft earth precursive of water. As if in redress for the unpalatable descent, the tired but happy path rolled back a curtain to present a happy ending. If she had owned a hat, she would have thrown it into the air. Right before her very eyes, a fetching mountain streamlet clear, cool, and clean, spouted merrily over a rock shelf into a catch basin.

Removing the foul-smelling boot necklace and unhitching the thirsty canteen from her belt, she knelt before the old ponderosa-hewn canova and lapped to fleshly replenishment and emotional consolation. For good measure she joyously splashed cool water over her sunburned face and hands. Lastly, daring to unlock the stubborn door to uncontrolled human behavior, she lifted her skirts and stood in the crumbling old basin, letting her stone-bruised feet rub each other in cleansing comfort. The foot bath inspired an upreach of the salubrious exercise, and making sure nobody was peeking through the bushes, she extended the bath to include the thighs, and even immodestly higher.

After what one might call ceremonial purification, she felt the need of an interlude of relaxation. Nearby, was a grassy mound where she was able to stretch out, and yet look down beyond the talus of the escarpment into a broad, hot plain. Although visibly extending at least ten miles, it encompassed nothing of encouragement. No mother stream was down there to capture the run-off of snow melt from the distant white-beaked mountains and pass it on to greater streams and greater dreams. Contemplating the futile errand of precious little stream that had given her a much needed interlude of healthful cleanness, a shadow fell across her heart for she knew it was doomed. After making its joyous way to the scorched plain below, this precious little watercourse would spread out over an arid playa and evaporate.

Her shadow spoke. She acknowledged its reminder of the hour with a nod. While the canteen refilled, she tugged up, washed, and pocketed edible roots and bulbs to add to her food bag. Then, rehanging the boots about her neck, she departed.

By the time she had clambered back to the rim of the canyon and geared for pursuit of the ongoing trail, the sun was getting ready to retire behind a purple facade of far-off mountains. In a little bit the western sky took on a pleasingly curious look of mingled copper and blue that all too soon became milky opal and then pearl. Evening then spread its gentle wings over the prairie, tolling an end of the day's occupation. As a rule at this hour, she would have begun looking for a suitable place to make her bed, but being energized by the visit to the mountain streamlet, she felt inspired to walk on for a spell, maybe for just a mile or two, depending on the legibility of rut creases.

Reading the trail was no problem, though, for some select stars from the galaxy's brightest and best hung lanterns in the grizzly sky, signaling their cohorts to light up. They did, flooding the high plain with an eerie whiteness, making it seem as if there had been a snowfall. As she pursued the trail, she reckoned if she had anything to read, she could read it, it was that light.

Presently there was a sky-change. A great, bright arch spanned the northern Heavens horizon to horizon. After flickering a few seconds, it sent spaced yellow-green rays upward toward the zenith. A native of the high plains, she was conversant with the dramatic behavior of the northern lights. Just the same, their unearthly manifestations always gave her the shivers, reverberating, no doubt, from an experience when she was nine and a half, maybe ten. Everybody in both dugouts had gone to bed that night when she was suddenly awakened by Tiger, her cat, fretting and scratching at the door to get out. She got up from her cot and opened the dugout door, abruptly coming face to face with what could only be the end of the world by fire, like Grandma's scriptures had prophesied. Screaming with fright, she woke up the whole family sleeping in both dugouts and elsewhere—all except Cousin Cooter.

Jule, sleeping naked in his bedroll under the wagon, was the first to respond. Pulling his pants on as he rolled out from under the studebaker, he hollered, "What's the matter? What's the matter?"

Grandpa, sleeping on a cot back of the dugout because it was too hot in the barn, reached for his shotgun and fired both barrels just in case. Cojo began to howl, and general pandemonium ensued.

When it developed that all the uproar got started when Leaf got scared of "them old lights that were as harmless as the moon," she was informed in no uncertain terms to shut up and go back to bed and let the family get some sleep. There was work to be done in the morning.

Back on her cot in the corner of the dugout, she shut her eyes so she wouldn't see those awful lights through the north window, but she didn't go right to sleep. The last thing she heard came from Jule. On his way back from the privy, he stumbled over Cousin Cooter's feet.

"Son-of-a-bitch!" he swore. "Damn near made me fall. I didn't know you'd come in."

With his head on a log at the woodpile and a bottle at his side, Cooter had slept through the whole commotion. He had walked fifteen miles after work so he could spend Sunday with his folks, the onliest folks he had anymore.

As time went on, she had learned to accept the exercise in magniloquence displayed by the aurora borealis as just that. Even so, she always breathed a sigh of relief when the show ended, as it now had.

Although she realized she was extending her night walk beyond the bounds of good sense and habit, she passed up several likely camping spots. She was wide awake, in the mood to walk and think, and the road was clearly readable in the eerie, stellar glow. So why not?

It was on a night like this so many years ago that she and Virgil had spread their saddle blankets on a starlit clearing and slept in each other's arms. They had ridden all day and into the night to reach a little sheep ranch that they hoped to buy and did buy. But not right away. Thus intruded old memories, memories that perforce she had been able to keep off limits by employing a stubborn cunning, alien to her nature but essential to her sanity. But sometimes they sneaked in and leeched on. Then all she could do was open the door to self-pity and cry on fate's shoulder.

Then it happened. Maybe it was a good thing that it did, because her human soul was on the verge of becoming submerged in the noxious atmosphere of despondency over a woman's place on this planet, where she had to occupy an intermediary role somewhere between animal and man. The extraordinary behavior of the trail automatically deferred the problem of a woman's rights to a day of reckoning on the Fifth Mesa.

It was unbelievable. Without so much as a how-do-you-do, the trail spread five fingers, insinuating in as many directions into the gray shadows of mesquite, rabbitbrush and darkness. By starglow, she anxiously probed for the explanatory sign post required by the humanitarian law of the trail. Finding none, and suddenly feeling weary, she began poking around for a place to lay her bed and leave the solution of the problem to the light of day. Too pooped to be choosey, she followed the stink of cow chip ashes to a small ring of stones where some previous pilgrim had recently slept.

Spreading the aristocrat of Navajo blankets and rugs, trade-named for the reservation settlement where patterned, dyed, and woven, she uncapped the menthol jar and turned in. Being very tired, she just laid there looking up at the pure white stars that hung down low, real low, turning the silent dove-gray prairie into a vast bed of lillies. Were they trying to tell her something? Had they the key that would unlock the door to deeper human understanding and wisdom, which would reveal a human being's naked reality to its true self, about whom it knows so little? Did the stars hold that one eccentric piece that once on the board would let the other pieces fall into place, providing the answers to the enigma of Truth, the reasons for human loneliness, pain, hunger, grief, and the inquisition of Time, that strange force that sentenced all life to death at the moment of birth, sometimes before? Did the stars know where the answers were stored? Could they give the direction?

Her startled eyes caught the trajectory of a luminous streamer as it arched the dome of Heaven, and pointed its downward cone toward the western horizon, a few degrees south. And she knew which of the five branching paths she should pursue on the morrow—the one leading west by south. She could sleep now. Pulling the corners of the warm blanket over her head to shut out the annoying giggle of roving coyotes, she forgot the stars, the world, everything.

8

When she awoke, she knew she had slept full round, but something was out of kilter. Her hair was damp, and her blanket smelled like a wet goat. It was daylight and yet it wasn't. Unbelievably, here in the sun-blessed Land of Enchantment, a dismal, slate-colored mist obscured everything more than a stone's throw away.

She sat up, and using the tail of her blouse to wipe her wet face, wondered at what hour the dense earth-cloud had moved in. All had been starry and clear when she had closed the books, so it must have sneaked up around midnight. It really didn't matter. In her entire life she had never known a completely sunless day, so she figured the depressing opaqueness that precluded her shadow from setting direction would soon dissipate. Actually, come to think of it, she had witnessed a heavy mist like this once before. Eight, no wait, it was easily ten years ago that she had been temporarily fogbound in the vicinity of Stanley, not far from White Lakes. That time the trusty old New Mexico sunshine melted the fog away muy pronto. She was sure it would do it again.

In the meantime, she crumbled a few leaves of Mormon tea in a cup of lukewarm water from the canteen that had slept at her feet. Sipping tea and nibbling pinon nuts, she waited for the dense curtain to roll back so she could determine which of the five trails headed west by south. The fog, however, thickened instead, limiting vision to less than twenty feet. This was discouraging. The unhappy situation might obtain for hours, precious hours needed for travel. So she decided to try to seek out the west-south arm of the trail designated by last night's meteor without the sun's assistance.

On the chance that in the starglow of the night before she had overlooked some sort of directional signal, she probed for the mist-hung hub from which the five byroads radiated, but all she found was a charred stub protruding from a base of ashes. Now she knew the story. The faithful multi-arm sentinel had surrendered to the sparks from Thor's hammer. Well, that took care of that! She would have to sit the fog out.

Most strangely, however, this was not necessary. An armless black hand emerged from a tuft of teary globe mallow, fingering its myopic way across the dewy grass, ready to pounce and feed. Her spirits soared. She stamped a decisive foot, and the spider quickly ran to the safety of his nearby web-lined hole, whose trap door always faces south. Thus, directions were established.

Pursuing the west by south road, she passed the time of restricted vision by counting steps. Eighteen hundred, give or take a few depending on the terrain, should approximate a mile. When she had covered some five miles, an opalescent glow appeared over her left shoulder. Presently, an ineffulgent disc of sun, a great pearl button, showed through a gauzy veil of weakening mist.

The dreary shell began to crack, first here and then there, exposing swatches of turquoise sky. Soon all was blue, clean, lucid, and the tangential silhouette of Leaning Rock stood out on the horizon in polished optical clarity. Peer though she might, however, her eyes could not descry any trace of the enchanted mesas. Overpowered by the insistent brilliance of the midmorning sun that seemed to be trying to make up lost time, the great listing landmark receded into bright distance.

Later the plateau began gradual relinquishment of its lofty command. The road plowed a downward furrow, while the gently respiring gramma yielded to knot grass and snakeweed, and the stately yucca stalks gave way to creosote bush and ragged, mouse-colored sage. Intervally, the countenance of the deteriorating terrain became pocked by ill-begot volcanic spittle, the color of dried blood. It looked as if an evil eye had been visited upon the route the trail had undertaken.

With the appearance of a series of raw gullies, the inhospitable area became more frustrating. While easing her way along a switchback laid out to accommodate footing across a particularly uncooperative arroyo, she paused to blow and contemplate the hapless plight of scrub cedar. The ill-favored little tree was forced to grow horizontally from roots crannied into an earth-chinked crevice in a sheer wall. Her heart reached out to the pathetically sprawling cedar with an emotion one carries deep in his human soul, unaware of its existence until a tear starts. A human being and a tree should be free to enjoy their natural heritage of upright growth, and not be reduced to the life-while of a snake or a vine—unless, of course, by choice. Some forms of life seem to prefer grovelling.

In the case of the laterally-growing cedar, she figured that nature, in its rigidly attuned pattern and rhythm, had pulled a boo-boo. It sometimes does, you know. Still, one should not quickly blame nature, unless the totality of its competence be held to embrace the behavior of man. Once upon a time good grass had grown knee high here, wild flowers had bloomed, seeded and bloomed again. But within the century this abundant land had been subjected to commercial overgrazing and overcultivation. Without a vegetized cover, the top soil blew away, erosion set in, and raw reptillian gullies were cut by flash floods. Surviving life had to hang on the best way it could, even if it meant growing sidewise from a hunk of soil caught in a crack in arroyo wall. And for Christ's sake, for whose good? With the shrine of revelation now within reach, she realized there was no point in becoming exercised over unanswerables, so she calmed down and filed the question among others she would put forward in audience with the Fifth Mesa.

In the meantime, the unpalatable terrain came to know beautiful weather, excessively beautiful. The earth was smiled upon by a favorable sun and fanned by a gentle, yet invigorating, breeze. Being an old timer, however, she had the feeling in her bones that there was something overbold about the total environment, something too good to be true.

The suspicion was well-founded. About midday, the sun turned its power up to the last notch. She was never so hot in her life, and not a gourd leaf in sight. Her hair gummed up and her eyelids narrowed to briny, oozing slits. Drops of funky sweat starting at her waist, maybe even higher, slimed embarrassingly all the way down, and there really was no modest way to blot them. Feeling miserable, to say the least, she began casting about for a respite of shade.

The only thing that showed up was a runty juniper so droopy and drought striken that it hardly seemed worthwhile to bother with. She was about to pass it up when she saw a pair of hunched gray jackrabbits, eyes closed, ears down, resting in a solid patch of shade, unnaturally cast from the fragile, upper branches of the tree. Sensing her presence, the dozing rabbits raised their flexible hearing devices and loped off.

The way cleared, she released her wooly burden that had come to smell like rancid butter and peered into the juniper's sparse, sagey limbs for whatever cast the shady spot that was about the size of a man's sombrero. She discovered an abandoned nest of grasses and twigs, deceptively woven into the juniper's topmost branches.

She couldn't tell whether the nest had been made by a hawk, a crow, a tree squirrel or what. Not that it mattered whose architectural prowess had been employed. The main thing was that the entangled mat deflected the merciless rays of the sun. Opining that a little bit of shade was better than none, she hunkered down under the tree's spread skirts, maneuvering her frame into the splotch of coolness inhospitably taken from her friends the jackrabbits in contravention of her native respect for the rights of others. Face was saved somewhat when she observed the pair snugly settled in tandem in the slim shadow of an old cedar fence post a few yards away. It was gratifying to know the rabbits would not be too uncomfortable until they could reclaim their shady nook after her departure.

She realized they wouldn't have to wait long. The cramped position she was forced to maintain in order to get a bit of shade made the reward scarcely worth the effort. More discouraging was the realization that having forgotten she was allergic to juniper pollen, she began to sneeze. She crawled out on hands and knees.

Once on her feet, she felt much better, or maybe she just imagined so because it was such a relief to get shed of that juniper. She let out a whopping kerchoo that splattered the landscape, but it sure cleared her nose of juniper dust.

This time, she maneuvered the Two Grey Hills to swing from a strap across her forehead. In uneasy but compelling compromise with decorum, she upped the posterior of her skirt, swinging the wide, velveteen gores overhead and out into a hand-supported canopy. Proceeding in this posture, albeit ready to drop the skirt at a moment's notice, she was able to deflect the sun's scorching glare to a considerable degree. The backlash was almost as discomforting, though. Her skin shrank from the breath of sudden shade, goose pimples broke out over her body, and the straw-colored hairs on her suspended, bare forearms bristled like ant feelers.

The surprising disparity between the temperatures of sun and shade revealed a much greater altitude than she had supposed. Maybe as much as a mile and a half. Pretty soon there was a leveling off, however, and she felt better. She made lively progress in the shelter of the velveteen awning until slowed down again by another, silty, rock-bedeviled arroyo that swallowed up the delineations of the trail. The only way she could keep track on this crooked, gravely course was by following animal droppings. After a while she became so absorbed in spotting waste matter that she took scant notice of certain behavorial changes of the elements.

Out of the blue came a powerful thunderclap, a real cream clabberer. She nearly jumped out of her skin, and the ruffled velveteen canopy automatically dropped. Not satisfied with splitting the sky wide open, the tater wagon rumbled across the startled earth. Quickly reading the sky, she observed over her right shoulder a dark cloud dripping like an over-absorbed sponge. It appeared to be about a mile or so to the east, and with a southwest wind against it, there didn't seem to be anything to worry about. But suddenly the wind switched to the east, a flash of lightning needled the ink-sotted cloud, and a second thunderclap applauded. The turgid cloud burst its seams, releasing a visible waterfall. It looked like grain pouring out of a slit sack.

A peculiar climate presently made itself felt, and she wondered in which direction the Rio Grande lay. Instinctively, she left the arroyo bed for higher ground. Clambering to the helmet of a nearby tinaja, she occupied a ringside seat, and not a moment too soon, for the overture was in progress. At first the chorus was muted like a distant buzz of blue bottle flies. Then, with the increasing tempo of an advancing army of overwrought teakettles, came an active hubble-bubble. In rapidly progressive steps the voices of the oncoming flood became agitated, angry, violent. Then a crashing wall of clayey water charged down the arroyo, spilling over its banks, licking at the very base of the tinaja where she sat observing a sea where none had been.

During her lifetime, and it extended over quite a stretch, she had known a lot of flash floods, but she had never gotten used to the swiftness with which they came. And went. The brick-colored tide crested quickly and ebbed just as quickly. In taut fascination, she watched torrent change into stream, into rivulet, into trickle, into wet sand, into dry dust under the pressure of the hot sun.

The startling greenness the abrupt dousing had awakened in the drab limbs of the cholla, faded. The antiseptic, sickroom smell emanating from suddenly primed glands of the creosote bush lost spirit, and the new arrangement of uprooted sage, flattened rabbitbrush, and dislodged rocks, could not be told from the old.

Disposition of drowned bodies was swift and efficient. Encircling black-suited vultures with obscene red wattles under their mouth parts came down to tear apart and consume dead bodies of ground-squirrels, rabbits, and mice while the overhead sun glowed in approval. In a matter of minutes all was as in the beginning, and ever shall be.

Now she had to come to grips with a ticklish situation. At the height of the crescendo, she had watched at least three wooden trail markers being slam-banged down toward the Rio Grande. Moreover, the flood had obliterated the visual sequence of animal droppings that had identified the gravel-based trail. In order to proceed, and proceed she must, she had to figure out some way to keep on course, for this was no country to get lost in. She put on her thinking cap, the one with the pink celuloid whirligig on top, and arrived at an idea that just might be the answer.

9

Animals had followed this trail ever since they had legs to walk on, and ever since there had been juicy grass and roots to nibble on and pass. Although the droppings themselves had been eliminated, the radiant activity of the almighty New Mexico sun on water-flushed earth always extruded latent, uric vapors, as anyone who had ever raised livestock can testify.

Hefting the pack to her shoulders, again balancing its weight from the leather forehead band, she proceeded in a stooped, over-reverential position peculiar to certain participants in religious processions, but there was nothing of humility or obeisance in her posturing. She simply had to scent the trail as she walked, to follow her nose, in other words, until she came to the visible, readable trail. By this method she was able to keep on course all right, but the unnatural posture she was forced to assume in doing so, not only was fatiguing, but threw something out of whack in her lower back. Uncomfortable as the going was, she dared not stop to straighten up and blow. She was racing against time. The extruded traces of urine were becoming weaker and weaker. They were barely sniffable at times, and at forkings she was forced to get down on her knees with her head bowed as if to receive the guillotine in order to nose out the main route. After a mile or maybe a mile and a quarter the interlude of olfactory navigation ended. She came upon a bona fide trail marker, index finger and all. What a relief!

Although it still was much too early to turn in, she kept her eyes peeled for a suitable place to camp, for her back was giving her fits. When she came upon an agreeable, isolated area sheltered by a scrawny stand of jackpines, she decided to call it a day, no matter what the sun said. Letting her pack fall where it would, she cautiously eased her ill-used frame down on a decrepit old wagon seat, half-expecting it to collapse. It supported her weight, however, without the slightest spring-sag. Opining they didn't make wagon seats like that anymore, she relaxed and took a deep breath.

When the strain imposed by mental and physical fatigue eased up and she began to feel like her old self, she surveyed her friendly surroundings. There was no doubt about it. Here had been a stamping ground. The presence of any cluster of trees, no matter how scraggly, was a come-on for a wayfarer, especially in a desert clime. Itinerant occupancy over many years was evidenced by the available accommodations. The little stand of jackpines sheltered a smooth-topped rock table, and around it were weather-scoured sitting stones. Nearby, but not close enough so the smoke would bother, was a rock-enclosed fireplace containing the carbonized residue of many fires. She saw Grandpa, he was a younger man then, come through the pines with an armful of wood, saw him lay it across the stones, strike a lucifer and blow. Memory trailed off at that point and was lost.

Immersed in probing thought, she fished in the deep waters of the past, and she got a bite. A sudden sensory impulse sent her down a narrow, weedy path, and she was reminded that she must watch out for the overreach of a certain fishhook cactus. As she knew it would, the path led to an abandoned, old corral, haphazardly enclosed by a fallen wall. Nearby, half-burried in weeds, lay a broken wagon wheel. Poking about, she uncovered a cracked singletree, a rusty U-shaped clevis that at sometime or other had dissolved partnership with a wagon tongue, the fractured cantle of a Spanish saddle, and the friendly noose of a hackamore— all lying half-submerged in time, weeds, and memory. Yes, memory, for she had been here before.

Gathering her skirts, she took a seat on a hunk of broken wall, unintentionally dispossessing a little collared lizard who skidaddled on hind legs in the posture of his ancestor, the dinosaur. The book of memory was wide open, and a timeworn page among the ABC's of life's recordings told her that this place, indeed, was part of valid experience. Memory went careering down the steep gradient of time with no brakes.

Clad only in the little flour sack drawers with Grandma's tatted lace around the leg holes, the garment in which she had slept on the wagon seat the night before, she was riding Grandpa's shoulders. He was young then, not yet forty, erect, strong, and darkly handsome (his mother was part Choctaw), and she, who couldn't have been more than three and a half, rode high and proud, holding on to a long lock of straight black hair. They were going down the path to the corral, where he would hitch up Grover and Benjamin who were in hobbles outside the barricade eating a breakfast of fresh green grass.

Suddenly Grandpa stopped. She heard a shaky noise, like gravel being sifted out of dry beans. She saw the snake wind up like it was throwing a ball and she saw it strike.

Grover Cleveland didn't say a word. He just looked at Grandpa. She knew, like little ones know, that something bad had happened, and she clung to her grandfather's neck, but he put her down anyway, making her sit on the rock wall, just about where she now sat. She was terribly frightened, but too absorbed in what was going on to cry. She watched Grandpa take out ahead of the rattler, which had unwound itself and was heading in a straight line for its hole. Grandpa beat the snake to the hole and stopped it up with a boot heel. Quick as a wink, he stooped and grabbed the thwarted critter by the tail, swinging it around over his head like a lariat. Then, cracking it like a quirt, he tossed it aside, dead as a door nail.

Taking his barlow out of his overall pocket and springing the blade, Grandpa knelt and slashed the flesh on Grover's front leg just above the hoof. He squeezed out a lot of mule blood and then spat Brown Mule tobacco juice into the wound. Next he cut the rattles and the button off the snake's tail and put them in his pocket for luck. Lastly, he hung the limp body of the rattler across the wall, with its scaley white underbelly upward so it would draw rain.

Grandma, she was young and lively then, called out, "Rufus, you and Baby come. Breakfast's ready." Memory drew a blank at that point. She knew, of course, that Grover Cleveland had survived to die of old age.

Returning to immediacy, she went back to the time-rubbed stone bench and rested her elbows on the rock table where they must have eaten breakfast that morning so many, many years ago. Her head drooped, her eyes closed, and she was not alone. Some came in breechcloth and feathers, others in velvet and gold, followed a man in a loose homespun robe, bearing a cross. Whiskered and tattered, they came with pickaxes over their shoulders, leading burros. Then came a new breed, big men with determined jaws and wide-brimmed hats shading their steely eyes. With them were the guarantees of survival, their womenfolks in poke bonnets, fingerless mits, and ankle-length alpaca skirts. The men read from the Bible and spoke of the land of milk and honey ahead, ever ahead, and the women sighed and hoped to God it was so. Life was mighty, mighty hard on the pioneer woman. Boys and girls, taciturn miniatures of their papas and mamas, crowded around the campfires, making out ghosts and goblins in the leaping flames, listening to the words of their elders in respectful silence. Children were to be seen, not heard, at that time, anyway. She watched the itinerant campers douse their fires, rake dirt over the hissing embers, and move on into the vast wilderness of hope, of reward, of fullfillment, of disappointment. Those she bade Godspeed were the growing pains of an infant civilization, one with far to go.

She thought what peculiar things dreams were. You don't know you have had them until they and you separate, and there is no calling them back for retelling. Yet they can roll back the somber curtain of distance and time, letting you revisit loved ones who have gone before, letting you feel their presence, talk to them, see them "through a glass darkly."

Her visit to the old campground in the jackpines begat what Mama used to call a "touch of the blues." Memory wore a black band on its sleeve, stirring the wellsprings of her conscience, reminding her as is the nature of one's conscience, of "what should have been," the eternal presumption in life being that the "should have been" would have turned out a lot better than the "did." But then, who could say?

On this evening of meditation, she felt deep rapport with her people, whose lives, especially in her childhood, had often been fraught with poverty and desperation. A certain year, her ninth, loomed bold on the horizon of memory. It was a year of scantiness and death. They had come hand in hand that year when she was nine, and she had never played with dolls again.

No crops were harvested at all that year. Hoping and sometimes even praying for rain, the menfolk plowed and harrowed the dry earth until it was as neatly groomed as a show horse's mane. Seeds were sown, and some of them even came up in the loosened soil, only to be blown over to the next county by the wild southwest winds.

No rains came. Oh, they favored other localities all right. Blue-bellied clouds turmoiled over the horizon, lightning flashed, and the tater wagon's hollow wheels rolled across the land. Visible pen strokes of water slanted from the dark, turgid clouds. But all we got was a picture.

Drought-stricken homesteaders gathered at the schoolhouse and solemnly prayed for rain. The Pueblo Indians put on a rain dance, and lo and behold, the wind switched to the east and a dark cloud moved overhead! But maybe the nesters didn't pray hard enough, or the Indians didn't dance fast enough for only a few bold drops splashed down to make little mud craters on the hard earth. That was all.

43

So many families pulled freight that her father's school closed again. The Lone Star Livery Stable in town laid off Uncle Jule, Cousin Cooter lost his job wrangling at the Cross L, and Granny took to her bed again.

Our neighbors, the Easterwoods, who liked to sing, didn't come over anymore. The two families used to sing old ballads at our place because we had an organ. Daddy held the lamp while Mama played the chords, and everybody sang the sad lays of Barbara Allen, Kitty Wells, and one that went—Lord Lovell stood at castle gate a 'combin' his milk-white steed, when up stepped Nancy Bell. But one day the Easterwoods loaded up their wagon and drove off. The rest of the family, especially Grandma, missed the Easterwoods. I didn't miss the young Easterwood at all. It made me feel all dirty when his hands tried to feel me when nobody was looking, but I was too ashamed to tell anybody. So, I was glad to get shed of him before I had to confide in Jule. There would have been a fight, maybe a killing.

Anyway, singing is not singing if you have to do it in the dark, and there wasn't any coal oil for Grandma's lamp. The lamp was an heirloom. She had held it on her lap all the way from Texas while the wagon wheels bucked gulch and gully. It used to be when the hand-painted Cherokee roses on the pale yellow globe lighted up, Granny's eyes lighted up too. But not anymore.

A family had to have the spondulix to buy coal oil, and we didn't have it. Grandpa sadly lamented that he would have to poot in his pocket to raise a cent. Nobody went to bed hungry, though, unless he just couldn't stomach fried rabbit anymore. We had to skimp on cackle berries and milk because they could be traded at the Murdock store for necessities like coffee beans, lard, flour or meal, and Brown Mule, a cheap chewing tobacco, which was cut up into rationed cuds. Luxuries like kerosene, sugar, soap, and Lone Star plug had to await better times. I missed the high class Texas chewing tobacco more than anything, because the men always gave me the silver stars embedded four to the plug. I wore them stuck to the front of my apron until they fell off. But actually, we never went hungry.

Of an evening after Granny, who was gradually going down hill, was tucked in, the rest of us used to sit on the settlebench outside Grandpa's dugout door or hunker down on the hard, bare earth and watch for lamps to come on in neighboring shanties and dugouts. During the initial in-rush of homesteaders, the plains used to light up like a big, spread-out town, for the land was so level you could see litten windows for eight or ten miles. But as bleak years went by, fewer and fewer lights came on after sundown. A litten window at night finally became a rarity and a subject for speculation.

"That there light over yonder must be at the Terry place. Wonder if somebody ought to ride over there and see if someone is sick."

Times didn't get any better. A lot of folks took to burning cow chips in the cookstove, but we never came to that. Grandpa was the boss and he said stinking a place up with Hereford coal was about as low as anybody could get, unless it was to gather bones. As time went on, however, a compromise with the family dignity was worked out in regard to the second taboo, bringing to mind the saddest of all days.

The chapter reporting what happened on that fateful day in her young life

44

had been reread so many times over the long years that her fingers opened her youthful biography at the proper page without direction. It was a tear-stained page, for before the story ended, the family circle would be broken.

BONES AND THE REAPER

One morning while Mama was buttoning up my apron, she looked out of the high dugout window and said, "Hon, I think the men are acting peculiar, like maybe they're up to something. Why don't you saunter out there and see if you can figure what it is?"

Exposure to Mama's curiosity was catching, and itching from it, I picked up a buttered biscuit and nonchalantly strolled out to where the men were monkeying around the wagon, building up the frame and palavering about something that had an air of privacy. Mama was right.

Our menfolk, like all I ever have known, never liked for the females of the family to butt into their affairs, so I sauntered toward the wagon, trying to appear unconcerned about what was going on. Bluebell, my pet black pullet, came up pleading from a sidewise eye like a hungry chicken does. Breaking off a piece of biscuit, I threw it in the direction of the wagon, keeping eyes and ears alert while I moved in to watch while Bluebell pecked it up. Then picking her up and lovingly stroking her shiny, black feathers, I edged even closer to where the men were building the wagon bed into a rack. Before long I had heard enough of their palaver to know they were pretty sure they could take the wagon out on the prairie and do the "job" without anybody being the wiser, but the real problem would be to get the load to town and collect the dough without being identified.

Seeing Mama's inquisitive face at the east window gave me the spunk to move in even closer, close enough to hear Uncle Jule say that tarped and still, the load could be passed off as hay, but the rattle would be a dead give away.

"DEAD give away is right," jested Cousin Cooter, who could make something funny out of anything. Jule and Daddy laughed and so did I, for I knew what was up. I went over to the window and told Mama, "They're goin' ghoulin.'"

45

10

"Is that all it is?" Mama said, as she turned to answer a call from sick Granny. Wondering why Mama sounded so relieved, I hurried back to where the men were.

"We got to get organized," Grandpa said impatiently as he hoisted the top sideboard up to Daddy. "Somebody's got to set there on the wagon seat and drive right through town and listen to them jackasses laugh."

"I can just hear 'em," Jule said. "So that uppity Bagby oufit are prairie ghoulin' after braggin' they would starve to death and go to hell first."

"My back is botherin' me again," Grandpa complained.

Daddy said, "Even if you sneaked the wagon by the bystanders, you'd still have to give your name to the tallyman at the boneyard, and that would be like putting it in the newspaper."

"Do I hear a volunteer?" Grandpa asked.

Jule said, "Hell, if I can shovel horsedung for a living, I guess I can drive a bone wagon."

"No," Cooter announced. "I haven't been with the family long enough for anybody in Melrose to know me. I can drive the load of bones right down the middle of main street and nobody will know me from Adam's off-ox. And if anybody says 'Ain't that the Bagby rig?' I'll just shake my head and drive on."

That settled it.

Then and there I made up my despotic, infantile mind to escape the awful dreariness at home by going bone gathering with the men. Still holding Bluebell, I approached Mama, who was hanging sick Granny's freshly-washed night clothes on the line back of the dugout. I told her I thought it was my duty to go along to drive the mules. That would free Grandpa to work from the ground along with Daddy, Jule, and Cooter.

"No!" Mama flatly said, as she picked up the empty clothes basket.

I followed her back to the dugout door, pleading my case. "I'm a good driver. Everybody admits that. And with me driving and the four men picking up the bones and throwing them in, the quicker the wagon will be filled and the sooner we can get back home and tarp the load so no one will know."

Before Mama opened the dugout door to go down, she said, "You listen to me. I simply cannot be left alone with Ma being out of her head so much of the time. If the worst should happen, there has got to be someone here to run for help. You are NOT GOING. And put that hen down! Mites are working all over your hands."

Mama's reasons why I should stay at home were the very ones driving me away. I could not tell her or anyone about that awful picture entitled, "The Grim Reaper Cometh" I had found in an old magazine. I had taken it to Grandma and asked who it was. She had put on her specs, and looking the picture over, she had said, "Why that's Death!"

In a way I felt sorry for Mama, but in a more compelling way, I knew I just could not be there when that awful thing wearing a hooded black robe and carrying a scythe over his shoulder opened the door. It was just too scary.

I took my argument to Grandpa, telling him how helpful it would be for me to go along to drive the wagon from one buffalo wallow to the next. He agreed, and spoke to Mama about it. But she put her foot down.

"Aggravatin' young 'un! She thinks because she's goin' on ten, she's one of the old blue hen's chickens. No, Pa, Leaf is needed here. That's all there is to it!"

I laid a plan, I watched Grover and Benjamin being hitched up, saw Daddy give Grandpa a hand to help him up to the spring seat, saw Daddy, Jule, and Cooter climb over the tail gate to stand on the floor of the wagon bed, saw and heard the iron-rimmed wheels turn and accelerate. Now was my chance. I tore out behind the moving wagon, grabbed onto the tail gate, and swung myself up into the wagon bed.

"Stop!" the men hollered and Grandpa put on the brake.

Daddy was furious. "Now, Miss Smart Aleck, you get right down from this wagon and go back to your mother!"

But looking back over his shoulder as he cinched the lines, Grandpa spoke, "If Hon wants to go that bad, she can go." Grandpa was the boss. He moved over to make room for me on the spring seat, and I triumphantly bounded to my prideful place at his side. But when the wagon slued to set out and I saw Mama standing there alone by the dugout door, knotting and unknotting her fingers in despair, my feathers fell. And yet, to my untaught, childish reasoning, that was the way it had to be.

With an empty, built-up wagon frame and a fresh team, the way across the trackless prairie was all rough and rattle. Daddy, Jule, and Cooter, jigging on the floor of the wagon bed, had to hold on to each other to steady themselves. When we got to the first old salt lick and slaughter hole, Cousin Cooter bounded out and gave his hand to Daddy. Grandpa handed the lines to me and accepted Jule's offer of assistance in getting down—his back was bothering again.

Fumbling through his jumper pockets, Grandpa produced some brown lengths of used, sleazy binder twine and passed them out. The men took turns tying each other's pants cuffs about the ankles so the centipedes living under the bones wouldn't slither up an overall leg to get' out of the sudden light. Then they got down to business.

From my perch on the wagon seat I reckoned I had never seen our men work any faster, even with a storm coming up. A foreleg, a hind leg, an armful of ribs were picked up like to much stove wood and quickly dumped over the endgate. What gave me the shivers was when a skull, fetched by a forefinger through an eye-socket, was hurled high over the side-boards and fell into the wagon with an unearthly clunk, for my mind's eye saw the wagon being hemmed in on all sides by thousands of undead buffalos who were itching for a chance to stampede the wagon in revenge for violation of the sacred resting places of their ancestors. History was one of my favorite subjects.

Then a funny thing happened—funny to all except Grandpa, and maybe Daddy. The mules got fooled. They whoaed before a field of white-faced, sand daisies that had somehow escaped the drought. Maybe having so much on his mind had a hand in it, but Grandpa didn't like our laughter. Climbing up to the end springseat, he took the lines from me and cussed the mules on, calling them nasty names. Very nasty. Fearful of a thwacking, the team struck up a jolting trot. But with a heavy load dragging on the traces and with Grandpa calming down, Grover and Benjamin settled back into a regulated, laborious plod—the life-gait of a contented mule.

Grandpa stayed on the sagging end of the springseat, his bulk making it even lower. I was still itching to drive the mules, but he only let me hold the lines until he lighted his corncob. I felt if I couldn't drive, I ought to get out and toss bones with the men, but I was barefooted, and pincushions were all over the place. Besides, I knew I would have to close my eyes when I touched a bone. So I just sat at Grandpa's side like a bump on a log.

In a little bit the wagon had all the ghastly cargo it could handle and then some. Flung bones, especially skulls, kept on rolling off and had to be picked up and thrown back. Jule and Cooter made a game of this. Jule would grab a fallen skull and hollering "Andy Over" to Cooter who was working on the other side, he would hurl the skull. Cooter would echo "Over" and catch the skull and try to tag Jule with it as they changed sides.

It looked like a lot of fun and I thought of asking Grandpa if I could be excused and join in, pincushions or not. But Grandpa, who was acting sort of nervous, stopped what he called "damn foolishness" and seeing that Daddy already was hitching a ride on the tail gate, he hollered, "Frank and me have had enough. Let's call it a day."

I sat there by Grandpa's side, thinking what an exciting day it was. The sunshine was deliciously warm, and bubbly white clouds rested in the deep turquoise sky. Everything seemed so right as the wagon wheels hiccoughed over clumps of turpentine weeds on the way home that I felt inspired to sing. Having just learned "Daisies Won't Tell" from Cousin Cooter who knew it and could chord it on the organ, I opened up "Sweet bunch of daisies brought from the dell . . ."

Grandpa turned toward me with a woebegone look on his troubled face that dispelled my inclination to vocalize. Sitting quietly at his side, sharing his gloom, I was haunted by a shamefaced feeling that wanting to sing at a time like this showed disloyalty to my family. Besides, I was so stupid I didn't know what a dell was anyway—unless it was a girl's name.

Pretty soon Grandpa's sternness softened. "They didn't mean nothin" he said. "I had no right to bless 'em out. I don't know what's got into me. Seems like ever time I turn around it's more trouble. The drought, your Granny's poorliness, and I jest heared yestiddy that the law says you can't shoot a Goddamn antelope without a permit. Now, who in the hell has got the money to buy a permit? Just the same, I shouldn't have blessed them out."

I cuddled affectionately against his shoulder. I knew all along that when he had cussed the mules for stopping at the little field of white flowers and we had all laughed, he didn't mean it. Many of a time, I heard Grandpa say, and say it from the heart, that Grover Cleveland and Benjamin Harrison were the best friends he ever had. And he didn't mean Presidents, either.

Cousin Cooter walked ahead of the wagon to stomp yucca stalks so they wouldn't drag on the coupling pole, while Jule walked behind to throw fallen bones back. Pretty soon, Cooter stopped and sighted across the horizontal prairie. Then, raising a palm, he signaled Grandpa to rein down. When Grandpa whoaed the mules to a halt, Cooter came alongside the wagon.

"Uncle Rufus, I think there's somebody out yonder. You see anything to the left about a mile ahead?"

Grandpa tied the lines around the brake and stood up, sighting under his hat brim. "I don't see nothin', but my eyes ain't so good. Give me your hand, Hon. Get up on the springseat and hold on to my shoulder. See if you can make out anybody, and if you do, try to see who it is."

All four of the men were at anxious hand when I stood up and sighted.

"It looks like Jimsam Strickland on Jupiter, but the way he's headed, he's angling away."

At the mention of the name of his sweetheart's father, Jule swung up to the rim of a front wheel. Holding on to the brake, he sighted and shook his head. "For God's sake, I don't want him, of all people, to see us." Carefully studying the distant moving horsebacker, he said, "You know, Pa, I surmise Strickland might just miss us. He ain't headed exactly this way, and he's so Goddamn nearsighted he can't tell his ass from a hole in the ground. If Jupiter don't whinny at our team, Jimsam may just keep on the way he's headed. 'Spose we all hold still for a few minutes so our sound won't carry."

The indifferent mules, the wagon load of bones, and the pride-lowered family who had gathered them quietly held still while Jule kept an eye on the fading form of the horsebacker. Pretty soon he said, "He's out of sight. Let's go!"

Mama met the wagon at the gate. Her face was as pale as a sheet and she was dabbing her eyes with a corner of her calico waist apron. She tried to tell what was the matter, but had to stop and cry before she could get it out. Finally, she snubbed back tears enough to mumble, "She thinks I'm Aunt Goldie." Then wiping her eyes and bracing her shoulders, she hurried back to the dugout and the irrational patient.

The men didn't say anything. They just looked woebegone while they worked fast throwing tarps over the bone wagon, cinching the gromets so nobody would think it wasn't hay.

"You all go in," Jule said, "I'll unhitch." Then Grandpa, Daddy, and Cooter took off their hats and went down into the dugout.

I put off going down, tagging after Uncle Jule while he unhitched the team and hung the bridles and traces on the hames. Then, swatting the mules' rumps, he sent them to the water tank and feed trough by themselves.

Placing a tender hand on my shoulder, he said, "Come on, Hon, let's go down."

But I was too scared. Picking Bluebell up, hugging the struggling pullet to my heart, I fled across the prairie, feeling strangely that I was running away from life as well as death, for on that day the two seemed entwined. I ran until I got short of breath and my side hurt. I stumbled and fell, and Bluebell got away. With glossy black wings outspread, she fled back toward the haven of the woodpile.

Getting up and removing a grass bur from the side of my right foot, I called out, "Cut-cut-cut Bluebell, Honey! See that old mean hawk circling up there? It's going to pick you up with its claws and take you off and eat you up feathers and all! I love you. Come back to me!"

But the hen kept on going, so I decided to run her down. When I was within some fifteen or twenty feet of her, she stopped. Turning toward me, she raised her head, arched her neck, and flapping her jet-black wings, uttered a terrible, un-hen sound. It was as if something had stuck in her throat.

Grandpa's bulk emerged from the dugout door. "I heared a hen crow. Where is she at? Was it Bluebell?"

Grandpa's voice was scary as all get out, but fearing for Bluebell's safety, I tried to be calm. "It wasn't Bluebell. It must have been some other hen. Look in the henhouse!"

Then, as if tempting the devil, Bluebell arched her neck again, raised her black silk wings, and released another bloodcurdling hen-crow, this one sounding sort of like a strangling horse.

"Shoo, Bluebell!" I screamed, but the confused pullet headed straight for Grandpa's crouching approach. He grabbed her by the feet.

"Please, Grandpa, let her go," I pleaded. "Bluebell didn't mean anything bad. Besides, she's mine. Grandma gave her to me. Please, Grandpa!"

"She crowed a death," Grandpa hollered in cold finality as he hurried toward the dugout carrying Bluebell upside down by the feet.

I ran after him. "You're hurting her. Put her down. She's mine. What are you going to do with her?"

Halting, he turned to me. "I'm goin' to do what you have to when a hen crows and somebody's sick. Come back with me. Your Granny is asking for you. And you can have your pick of any other chicken on the place."

I was mad as a hornet. "You could offer me a hundred other hens, and I'd say, 'Kiss my foot!'"

Wheeling, I fled from the ill-starred premises, not looking or caring where I was going, just running. Soon exhausted, I sank to the ground behind a clump of yucca where I would not be seen from the dugout. Burying my face in my arms, I sobbed until I fell asleep.

Later, I was awakened by Mama's high-pitched, "You-hoo, Leaf Marie! Come home wherever you are and see your Granny. She's all right now!"

Obediently, I got to my feet so Mama could see where I was. Spanking grass chaff from the seat of my calico apron, an old one of Mama's cut down, I walked back to Grandpa's big dugout across the road from our little one, which we rarely entered except to sleep.

When I got back I didn't go down. I just stood in the dugout doorway looking at everybody, puzzled by the atmosphere of cheerfulness. Granny, propped up on three pillows, her Bible in her lap, was reading aloud from the "begats." All smiles, Mama was setting the table. Grandpa, sitting in his old reed rocker, was calmly smoking his corncob, Jule and Cooter were playing pitch, dealing the cards out on an up-end cracker box. Daddy was stoking the cookstove.

"Miss Lizzie," he said. "If you keep on getting better, you can ride to town in the bone wagon and buy yourself something pretty."

Minding her place with an emaciated finger, Granny nodded approval and went on reading to the end of the chapter. Then, looking over her specs at Daddy, she reminded him, "Now, Frank, you know good and well what my name is. It is Elizabeth Ragsdale Bagby."

Everybody laughed happily.

"Ma's her old self," Jule promptly declared as he riffled the deck.

Looking down upon my beloved family group, tears of contrition welled, for I knew I had been a bad girl. Wiping my eyes on the tail of my apron, I started to go down the steps and join the circle, but I was stopped by a tell-tale smell. A sickening odor issuing from the half-buried room turned my stomach. It was not from Granny's bed, that sometimes smelled in spite of carbolic sprinklings. It came from the cookstove.

The lid on the black-bellied stew pot was dancing up and down, giving off a nauseaous vapor that sagged the cobwebs on the overhead rafters. My eyes seized on the slop bucket at the side of the step where I was standing. Floating on a raft of wilted black feathers and writhing entrails was a beautiful black silk head whose red comb roached aside to reveal a cold, sightless eye. A stilled gaping beak spat a small, clean tongue.

I reeled, but managed not to fall. I just stood there staring into the care-rutted face of my grandfather. Putting his pipe aside, he got up from his rocker. Holding out his great arms where curly black hairs showed through holes in his ragged shirt sleeves, he pleaded, "Come to your Grandpa, Hon!"

Shaking my head, I ran out of the dugout door and vomitted.

11

Mama, Grandpa, and Jule were at Grandma's side when she died around mid-night. Jule came over and knocked on our door to tell us. I put my calico apron on over my nightgown, Daddy pulled his pants on, and we went right over. I wasn't afraid with Daddy holding my hand. Anyway, I supposed the Reaper had already come and got Granny and taken her away. But she was lying there in bed with her head on the pillow, not looking a bit dead but more like she was asleep.

Mama said, "Hon, come and kiss your Granny goodbye before we lay her out. Cooter has gone to fetch Miz Bascomb to help." I must have cringed, because Daddy put an arm about my shoulder.

"No," he declared emphatically, "I'm going to take Leaf home and put her to bed."

Although I came nearly to his shoulder, he picked me up like I was a little thing. On the way to our own small dugout that wasn't more than a hundred feet away, he let me down and pointed to the twinkling overhead sky. "Miss Lizzie is up there in Heaven," he said. "Tomorrow we'll bury the shell she left behind."

I understood, and leaning against his shoulder, I felt closer to my father than ever before, although I was perhaps never to feel that close again.

After the funeral Mama found a letter in Grandma's Bible addressed to her husband and children, asking that they grieve not, because she was "going home." She also requested that the name of her marker not be "Lizzie Bagby" but "Eliza-beth Ragsdale Bagby." The name, as she wanted, was chiseled into the base of a marble statue of an angel bearing a cross on her shoulders, but not until the follow-ing year when it rained and there was money from crops.

Replacing Bones and the Reaper in the carapace built around old memories, she moved away from the haunted spot to look for a place to camp. She chose a fairly level spot, far enough away so the past wouldn't take possession. Her back was killing her, but she knew all it needed was a soft bed, and peace of mind.

After removing loose rocks and other incidental impedimenta from the staked out area, she gathered lapfuls of crisp, brown jack pine needles and strewed them evenly over the designated area. Over the needles she laid silken sprays of butterfly bush. The carefully spread Two Grey Hills completed the inviting ensemble.

Although her bones pestered for the bed, she refused to turn in right off. It was a rule as old time that a grownup never went to bed before sundown—unless, of course, coming down with a cold or something. So she sat on the readied couch chomping nuts and tubers, trying to keep awake until the copper-colored sun slipped behind a ridge of shadowy hills. As soon as it blew out the light, she unlidded the menthol jar, kicked her boots off, and submitted to the curative caress of the bed, the cordillera of her bones scarcely making a ripple on its surface.

Free of backache and lifted in spirit, she was well along in pursuit of her quest when the last pale asterisk blended into the dawning sky. And it was a mighty good thing she got an early start, for the trail undertook some rough country. Before her very eyes, the terrain became inhabited by all manner of badlands, innocent of vegetation but abundant in weird, up-thrusting limestone tents grouped in strange, silent communities reminescent of Biblical lore.

She meandered through chalky encampments of calcareous tent rocks with less physical than emotional strain. Then around mid-afternoon, the merciless clout of the sun forced her to take respite in the shadow of one of the outlandish, bone-colored tabernacles. Releasing the sweaty, woolen burden, she sat with draped cross-legs on the hard, windswept earth, letting her back rest against a precisely tapered wall.

The sudden, sweet shade was narcotic. She catnapped, awoke, and catnapped again. And again. Whether asleep or awake, she was haunted by an uneasy feeling of being under the surveillance of a suspicious nomad wearing a turban and a long sleeved white gown, with maybe a rifle under it. Watching her chance, she quietly slipped out of and away from the suspicious outpost. And not a minute too soon, for she had begun thinking about making a will.

Luckily, a more salubrious climate, both political and atmospheric, came to her rescue. The trail got shed of these barbarian tent rocks and the wind changed to the east. The weather was refreshingly mild as her way led across a semi-desert area where abundant cacti grew. Surprisingly, the dogear prickly pear had shed its roses, leaving spiculate thumbs of green tunas to ripen to garnet, and pretty soon now. Summer was just about done for. And where had it gone?

The situation clamored for immediate attention. Her schedule called for her arrival at Leaning Rock by the time the prickly pears were ripe, and they would be ripe soon. Although unred, they already had reached a period of maturation that made her gastric juices sit up and take notice. But where was the massive, genuflecting rock? Road signs dutifully assured that she was on the right track, but the monument itself had not been visible for days, maybe weeks. Maybe there had been an earthquake.

Getting hold of herself, she realized that letting a case of nervous fidgets get a foot inside the door would not solve anything. It would only cause a loss of time. Accepting the authority of rationality and good old common sense, she kept to the trail, and it was a good thing she was emotionally prepared to cope with what she encountered around the next bend.

She walked right up to a bed of the biggest prickly pears she had ever seen. Even though the raised thumbs of tunas were still unripe, the sight of them made her drool. Being consciously aware of her lack of visceral rapport with green prickly pears, she looked the other way, but knowing they were at hand made her lips smack even more.

Being of a conciliatory nature, she proposed that her appetite and the status quo work out a compromise. They did. And how they did! Employing the fine salvage thread from a yucca blade as a line, she lassoed two adjoining green pears, drawing them tightly together. Then, with a dash of Shakespearean villany, she quickly snatched the infants from their mother's suckle. Cautiously holding each immature pear between thumb and forefinger, she abraded the vicious nests of burgeoning spines on the soles of her boots. All told, she took twelve raw fruits, two from six separate plants. These she strung like beads on a yucca thread that carries its own needle. Lastly, she double-knotted the ends of the string together, contriving a circlet that she wore on her head, calculating that if the warm weather held up, the fruits on the tiara would be ready to eat in three days. And, by golly, they were!

And as she walked along tossing the delicious cactus pears in her mouth, chewing and swallowing the lucious pulp, she wished every hungry mouth in the world could share her treat. She didn't forget to spit the seeds for the birds.

As time went on, the fruitful level plain that the trail pursued failed to disclose certain plaguing obliquities of terrain. In cautiously negotiating with one of these unheralded dry washes, she came upon an old piece of plank that had been caught, God knows when, in a tangle of looping yucca roots. Looking the ancient board over, she figured it might well have washed loose from the Ark during Noah's tussle with the world's most celebrated gully washer.

Curiosity mingled with an innate obligation to subvert whatever entrapment, even though the charitable gesture often backfired, and she extricated the piece of decaying lumber from the clutches of the root mass. Studying it, she made the amazing discovery that she had seen it before. This old piece of rotten plank had once identified the north, no, the east, boundary of the prestigious Flying B. Ranch.

The crumbling old board carried more weight in memory than in substance, and she tossed it aside quickly finagling her way out of the dry arroyo. Back on the easy-going trail, she took down from the shelf, a certain volume blowing off an accumulation of dust, recalling as she blew that while the incident at the Flying B had occurred when she was barely thirteen, the impact on her life had not truly been revealed until she was a junior in high school, having at that time decided to become a great author instead of a circus acrobat.

INCIDENT AT THE FLYING B

It began when Mr. Rucker's RFD buggy brought our mail from Melrose on his weekly delivery. As a rule, he got to our place around two, Wednesday afternoon, and it was my prideful job to watch for the flag, an old bandana of Grandpa's, to go up over our wooden box that was nailed to a fence post at the intersection.

On this particular Wednesday, as soon as I saw the flag, I shoved my bare feet into my sandals because of grass burs and headed for the box. On thumbing through the contents to make sure all of it was for us, I discovered an important-looking envelope addressed to Mama, with the return address a capital "B" with wings. I quickly put the letter in my apron pocket for safety, and with Grandma's Christian Advocate, which still came although her address had been Heaven for close to four years, Grandpa's socialist Ripsaw, and everybody's Sears Roebuck catalogue—and it was about time, for the old one was down to the xylophones and zithers—I hightailed it back home full of excitement, because the B with wings was at that time the brand of the biggest spread on the Caprock plain.

A personal letter being a rarity, the arrival of one always stirred up a lot of family interest. This one from wealthy Clovis Bynum aroused so much curiosity that Mama had to nudge the others out of the way so she could rip the envelope with a fork without poking somebody in the eye. Daddy already had on his gold-rimmed specs in anticipation.

"Let me read it, Ethel," he insisted. "He would have sent it to me if he had known I'd come back."

But Mama wouldn't let go. "It's addressed to ME," she snapped. Clearing her throat, she read:

Dear Mrs. Whitfield:

I take my pen in hand on this 5th inst. (Daddy interrupted to explain that Bynum meant the fifth of the current month, which was August.) I address myself to you in regard to the possibility of your daughter, Leaf Marie, assisting my wife and our cook in chores relating to the noon meal for the harvest crew, when the thresher appears at my spread at nine o'clock on the morning of the 12th inst.

Miss Leaf will be expected to tote water, catch and help pick frying chickens, and attend to other chores as assigned by my wife or the cook. These will also include washing and storing dishes and silverware after dinner is over. For this service I offer to pay fifty cents.

If the above is agreeable to you, please let me know as soon as possible, so I will not have to make a second choice, for your daughter has been highly recommended by a teacher. In case of acceptance, please have Miss Leaf at my main house on Bynum Road by 9:00 A.M. on the 12th inst.

Very respectfully,
Clovis R. Bynum, Esq.

My enormously impressed relatives, all except Grandpa, who had druther see what Eugene Debs had to say, agreed that a letter of acceptance had to be sent at once, especially inasmuch as the flyblown calendar hanging back of the stove and bearing a full color picture of a fecund white-faced bull, warned that it already was the seventh.

Funning, but with a smack of truth, Jule said, "While our little gal eats high on the hog on the twelfth, it'll be musical fruit (Mexican beans) and cornbread for we'uns here who are as pore as Job's turkey."

Daddy shushed Jule, and Cooter, too, before Cooter could pick up his line and ask, "How pore was Job's turkey?" I knew why Daddy shushed them, and I appreciated that while Daddy and Mama disagreed on a lot of things, they were united in a serious endeavor to keep smutty language from the ears of their little girl. In this case, however, Daddy needn't have bothered. Ever since fifth grade, I, and the whole class, had known that Job's turkey was so pore he had to lean against the fence to do what the girls, most of them anyway, called doo-doo. All the boys, of course, used a shorter word, more to the point. But all that kid stuff was behind me now, and if Jule and Cooter had been permitted to go through their act it would have fallen on deaf ears. Although when you come right down to it, crude as Jule was, he was the one who taught me how to defend myself against the opposite sex.

"Frank, have you got a pencil?" Mama said. In mute reply Daddy turned both pockets inside out, like when he was broke.

"If I can just find that tablet that's got a pencil tied to it, you can help me with the letter."

"I'll say AMEN to that," Daddy agreed, needlessly emphasizing that Mama never got past sixth grade. But then, educated people act that way sometimes They can't help theirselves—I mean themselves.

Mama began turning the place upside down looking for a tablet with the attached pencil. I knew where it was, but I didn't speak up for two reasons. One probably the more compelling, was that I had drawn some pictures on that table that I didn't want anybody to see, especially Grandpa. This was because his half sister, Aunt Pet, drew, even painted, silly pictures and had had to be committed. Grandpa was sensitive about it. In the second place, although I was the party most concerned in the Bynum letter, nobody had asked me what I thought about it. Had anyone done so, I should have shown the enthusiasm I felt in my ambitious young heart, for nothing important had ever before come my way. Having been left out of the picture, I just sat there on a dugout step like a frog on a log.

Sensing the situation, Mama patted my head as she passed by to search sewing machine drawers for writing materials. "Aren't you excited about being so important?" Then almost, but not quite out of my ear range, she cautioned, "Leaf Marie is at that sensitive age."

Daddy, Jule, and even Cooter seemed to comprehend, giving me verbal pat on the back. Grandpa only said, "Make room, Hon, I've got to see a man about a horse."

I got up from the step to let him by. Then, reaching under it, I retrieved the tablet and pencil. Tearing out my silly drawings, especially one showing a tiny little mouse chasing a great big tomcat who was running for dear life, and stuffing them into my apron pocket to rip up later, I handed Mama the tablet.

Even before the sun went down on the eleventh, Mama began counseling me "Now eat a good supper and get to bed early. You're going to have a heavy day tomorrow. Be sure to ask your grandpa to wake you up."

Grandpa was poking the fire under the coffee pot. "Let her alone," he said "Have I ever forgot to wake anybody up in time? Quit actin' like a hen with only one chick."

Mama shut up and set the table. I sat down and flipped my plate, but I couldn't work up any interest in food. I just piddled around with my cornbread and beans, drank a glass of water, asked to be excused, and got up and went to the haven of your own small dugout. Not bothering to turn up the wick, I undressed and pulled my flour sack nightie over my head. Too tired to kneel, I crawled into my cot and dutifully prayed in one long word: NowIlaymedowntosleepIpraythe LordmysoultokeepIfIshoulddiebeforeIwakeIpraytheLordmysoultotakeAMEN. When Mama and Daddy came in, I aroused just enough to know they had stayed late in Grandpa's dugout to play coon can with the boys.

On the morning of the twelfth, I was awakened to the important day by a double rap on the dugout door, the wake up call of my grandfather, whose prideful duty not only was to keep the old Seth Thomas on the shelf over the washstand and the men's watches timed to the "shadder stick," but to alert any member of the family who had to meet an early schedule.

Mama had laid out clean underwear and a freshly-ironed denim apron for me so I dressed quietly and for the first time in my life, sneaked up the steps before my parents woke up. Closing the door behind me, I enjoyed a pleasing feeling that I was closing the door on all that apron string stuff only to hear Mama call, "Leaf! Leaf Marie! The lark is up—Where are you?"

Instead of going to the family wash bench back of the dugout, I went to the men's wash-up at the windmill. I had done this from time to time ever since I had started doing outside work, although Mama didn't like for me to because the men got awfully dirty, and besides, the windmill tank and its washstand were open to passersby, and you never could tell whether some of them had something catching.

Removing the rock we kept in the wash pan to keep it from blowing away, I filled the basin with cold water and scrubbed my face and hands with the soap-weed washrag kept in a nailed-down sardine can. I was drying off on the grimy roller towel hanging from a post near the wash place when Jule came up for his turn.

"I'm acquainted with Clove Bynum's Mexican-Chinese cook," he commented, rolling up his sleeves. "He's one of the interestingest critters I ever met. I used to play poker with him when he cooked for the Dirty Sow (the Delux Cafe). I still do sometimes, so I thought I'd drive you over the the Flying B and say 'howdy' to him."

"No, you won't," I snapped. "I'm driving myself!"

Surprised by what he called my sass, he jawed me and I jawed him right back. Any why not?

"Already for the past six months, I have been considered grownup enough to help with the milking, tote fodder for the cows, slop the hogs, and drive Mama to the Murdock store," I informed him.

"You don't know the way," he said.

"'course, I do," I yapped back. "I know every crook and turn on the way to Bynum Road, and you can see the big white house for miles."

"All right! All right! Have it your own way!" Throwing up both hands in exasperation, he walked away, muttering about seeing Sam on business. I couldn't help feeling satisfied that he had given in.

12

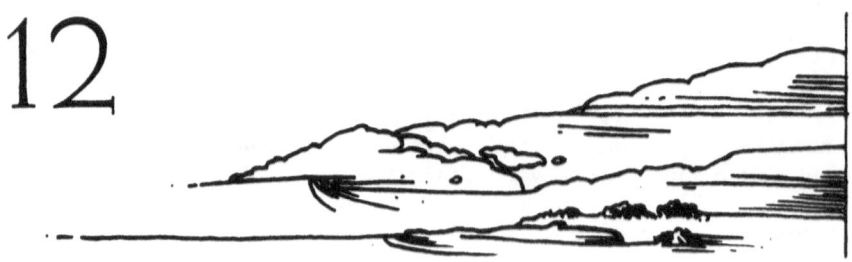

Jules' acquiescence bolstered my self-confidence to the extent that in further demonstration of my independence, I flatly rejected Mama's urgent suggestion that I eat up the oversize helpings of fried eggs and buttered biscuits she placed before me.

Grandpa hollered that the buggy was hitched up, and without a word to anybody I shoved my untouched plate back, got up and hurried out. Bouncing up to my seat in the buckboard, flapping the reins, I was off to a good start into a new world, a new life.

The sky was as blue as the wild asters that lined the road, the sun bright, the air gingery. Blackie was rested, full of feterita and mettlesome. Time and the wheels spun so fast that it wasn't long before I slowed and slued the buckboard over the rattling iron bars of the cattleguard onto Bynum Road that led up to the big white house and two windmills, one for the house and one for the stock.

Nearing the big house, I let Blackie blow, while wide-eyed I stared at the residence of a rich man. The whitewashed brick walls of the highly fashionable, territorial colonial mansion were set off at the top by a neat copping of reverse lying red bricks, reminding me somehow of an elegant lady wearing a white dress and a red hat. The total scene of the main house of the Flying B was even more impressive than the post cards I had seen of it on the drugstore rack. Wonderful to behold! Even more beautiful, I was to be a part of it!

Reining Blackie over to the first of a formal stand of hitching posts, I looped the lines over and proudly walked down the portal past a row of saddle racks laden with expensive Texas saddles with high saddlebows and flying B's branded on the flaps. Marching up to the hand-carved front door, smoothing my apron and straightening my hair, I raised a heavy brass knocker and let it fall. Nothing happened. In a little bit I did it again, only harder. This time, the sleepy voice of a woman called, "Who's there?" When I identified myself, she informed me where the kitchen door was.

Feeling like two cents, each with a hole in it, I went around to the back door. With considerably diminished self-confidence I knocked. I was unprepared for the sort of man who opened the door and extended his hand. "Me Sam Lee," he said. "You Miss Leaf?" I just stood there for a moment and then said, "Si, Senor," which along with "gracias" and "adios" was about all the Spanish I knew at that time.

Sam Lee did look a little bit Mexican and little bit Chinesey around the beany eyes, but his skin was light and he was sort of tall, like maybe he was part Californian. But mostly, he looked like any other cowboy. He had on a red and green plaid shirt, a wide-brim, dove-gray, stetson, and a turquoise bracelet which he took off and laid on the washstand shelf before he began shaking the grate of the biggest range I ever had seen, even in Sears Roebuck catalogues. After he had laid the kindling and struck the match, he looked up at me and grinned.

"Played poker all night. Boss had to eat breakfast at bunkhouse. Maybe get fired. Miss Leaf, take buckets to windmill tank. Need agua muy pronto."

When I got back with the double tote, Sam, his stetson still on, was gallusing into a white apron. He opened the lid to the bone-dry range reservoir and poured the water in. Then he sent me back to the Dempster tank. It took three double totes to quench the reservoir's thirst. Not only that, but it took another three to fill the drinking water tank in the pantry. Right off the reel, I ran my legs off and was ready to flop. Moreover, my innards were now griping because of no breakfast.

I sat down on a stack of firewood at the side of the stove, but not for long. Sam kept on telling me to hand him this and that, so I soon gave up trying to sit. Although he kept me on the run, I got along pretty well until he began preparing his mistress' breakfast tray.

The smell of frying bacon and scrambling eggs sent my gastric juices into flood stage. Wiping drool on an apron sleeve, I stood on one foot and then the other, trying to get up enough courage to throw myself on Sam's mercy and tell him I was starving. But courage doesn't come quickly when one is young. I just suffered. After he left with the tray, I inspected the cooking utensils for scrapings, but with no luck. Only grease was there. Fooling around, poking and smelling, I came upon a half-filled cream pitcher from which I took a great big swallow that lulled my appetite a bit, and then I juned around straightening the kitchen up, for I did want to be helpful and earn my fifty cents.

But when Sam brought the scarcely touched breakfast tray back, the lull was over. I was steeling up to ask him if I could have the leavings when he began scraping them into a yellow bowl. Opening the back door, he called, "Kitty-Kitty-Kitty! Come Pancho Villa!"

At that point, I came to grips with my miserable situation. I had either to get in the buckboard and head for home, or to grin and bear the situation. Sam made the decision for me.

"Miss Leaf, pretty name, got long strong legs. Me got rheumatism. Come with me. Maybe you catch chickens."

Following him to the poultry yard, I ran down and caught every chicken he picked out, carrying each struggling fryer to him, shutting my eyes while its neck was wrung. In all there were about a dozen. Holding each dead or dying chicken by its yellow feet, Sam dipped it in a copper-bottomed kettle of boiling water. Then, for at least an hour, I plucked stinking, soggy feathers off nauseating, scalded chicken flesh. The only good thing about it was that it quelled my appetite—at least temporarily.

Around ten thirty, maybe eleven, Mrs. Bynum, a plump, blond, middle-aged lady wearing gold-rimmed specs came into the kitchen. She acted real nice, "How do you do, Leaf Marie," she said. "Glad to meet you." We shook hands. She showed me the dining room, which was larger than our whole dugout. A long white damask table cloth already was on the table that was twice as wide and three times as long as ours. Opening the glass door of a mahogany cupboard, she showed me where the dishes, silver, and napkins were kept. After instructing me to set the table for twelve, she went back to the kitchen.

I didn't have a bit of trouble dealing out the twelve gold-rimmed plates, but I couldn't figure what to do with the knives, forks, and spoons. Beckoning Mrs. Bynum from the open door between the dining room and kitchen, I asked her what I was to put the eating utensils in? Looking the dining table over in bug-eyed surprise, she said, "Why are the plates upside down, Leaf Marie?"

I explained that at home we always placed the plates buttoms-up so the flies wouldn't speck them.

"I don't think we have to worry about that," she said, shaking her head in disbelief. "Now what was it about the silverware?"

Although somehow I knew it would make me appear even more countrified, I explained that at home we kept the knives, forks and spoons in a tin can in the center of the table and everybody helped themselves. Mrs. Bynum advised me to go into the kitchen and help Sam. She would take care of the table.

In spite of feeling taken down a peg, I was relieved to get shed of that la-de-dah dining room and be back in the active kitchen, where Sam was standing in front of the biggest iron skillet I had ever seen. I inched over to see what he was doing. He was using a long-handled fork to rotate pieces of chicken as they browned in bubbling grease, lifting done ones out onto an oversized platter. He sure was working fast. Beads of sweat were oozing from the damp headband of his hat, running down his brown cheeks, but he didn't stop to wipe on the roller towel until all the chicken was fried.

When he opened the sliding glass doors to the warming oven that would hold the chicken and other food until served, I caught a mouthwatering whiff of ham-seasoned blackeyed peas and felt I was going to faint. Moving out of Sam's way at his suggestion, "before you get burnt," I beheld half a dozen dun-colored pumpkin pies with neatly pinched crusts cooling on the wide window ledge. That did it.

Saliva driveled down my chin and my legs sagged. Staggering out of the kitchen door, I flopped on a bench alongisde a ten gallon galvanized milk can. I felt better away from the food smell, and I asked of myself, "When in tarnation did you eat last?" Come to think about it, not only had I passed up breakfast this morning, but I had refused to eat supper last evening. No wonder I was hungry as a wolf, but I reckoned that with noon dinner just about ready, I could hold out. Seeing a pan of water nearby and thinking a good drink would help me along, I picked it up and took a larruping gulp, only to learn from a couple of lop-eared dogs whose it was.

Sam came tearing out of the kitchen with a determined look in his beady eyes and a hammer in his hand. He gave me a funny look and I ducked around the corner and got set to kick him, you know where, like Jule had taught me to do to protect myself, especially from foreigners. I felt sort of sheepish, though when the cast iron bell clang-clanged. With the hammer loosely in hand, Sam hurried back toward the kitchen, motioning to me, and I followed him inside to help him fill the platters for passing.

In a little bit, a dozen or so hairy-armed, sunburnt harvest hands who had washed up at the windmill but still had thresher dust in their ears and hair, stood in a proper line while Mrs. Bynum showed them their places. Having my eyes peeled for a look at the wealthy Clovis Bynum, I couldn't believe my eyes, or my ears either when I heard Mrs. Bynum tell a chunky, red-faced man wearing dusty bib overalls like the rest, "Clove, you sit at the head." He sure didn't look like a rich man.

When he asked that heads be bowed and muttered a standard preacher's grace, I was even less impressed. How different it was when the thresher came to the Bagby place! These same harvest hands, smelling of uncut sweat and labor, found places on boxes, stools, and reinforced old chairs around the old dining table that had been set up under a sickly cottonwood in the front yard. When Grandpa signaled a lowering of heads, they would cut short their nudging and joshing.

Grandpa prayed, "Bless the meat and damn the skin. Flip yer plates and pitch right in!" Everybody hollered "Amen," and what a merry old time they had. I always did, too, because Mama let me pour the preferences. But now that I knew how it was in a well-to-do home, where a person never belched at the table, I wondered where I would stand to pour the preferences next harvest time? Would it be at the traditional fodder pitcher's table of ham hocks, turnip greens, and cornbread, or would it be where food was served on gold-rimmed plates? I wondered how much one of those plates cost.

But nobody asked me to do any pouring. Everything already was poured, and it wasn't buttermilk. And there wasn't any chair for me. I watched Sam serve everybody and followed him back to the kitchen, "Where's my place?" I asked. He didn't say a word. He just went back to the dining room and spoke to Mrs. Bynum, who was sitting at the foot of the table. Then he came back and took a pan of baked potatoes with skins on out of the warming oven. Holding it out, he said, "Miss Bynum says you take a potato and wait."

Confused, slapped-down, put in my place—a lowly one—I just stood there.

Sam was impatient. "Take a tater quick! Platter hot! Me busy man!"

Not knowing what else to do, I picked up a hot potato shifting it back and forth between hands until they could stand the heat. Suddenly feeling a cry coming on, I headed for the back yard, where I had seen a dangling old rope swing. Snubbing tears, still holding on to the cooling spud, I backed down on the wooden seat board, steadying the swing's awakened movement by pressing my feet on the hard earth. I must have sat there for five or ten minutes trying to get hold of myself, for inspite of the embarrassing turn of events, I was still hungry. Pulling back the wrinkling brown potato skin, I nibbled without relish at the tasteless white pulp. I was hungry for chicken, not taters, so I decided to throw the dang-blasted thing away.

At that moment a couple of Rhode Island Reds came up cautiously eyeing the tater and me, saying "cut-cut-cut" like hens do, especially ones having Rhode Island blood and most of them have because of so many Rhode Island Red roosters. Breaking the uneaten potato into equal parts, I threw the pieces to the chickens, and with good riddance.

Then twisting in the swing, I sit-walked around and around like I used to do at school at recess, making the guy ropes twine together as far as they could go. That done, I struck both legs straight out and let the released ropes dizzily unwind. Very little giddiness, resulted, perhaps because I no longer was a child. So I quietly sat on the swing seat letting my feet fool around on the ground while the cat died, thinking—thinking and feeling like Grandma's Biblical stranger in a strange land. I was the stranger and the Flying B was the alien land where everybody ate chicken, black-eyed peas, and pumpkin pie, everybody, that is, except a little girl who was told to take a tater and wait because she was poor folks who lived in a dugout and ate beans and cornbread.

So immersed I became in my depressing situation that Sam had to call twice, the second time real loud, for me to come in and help with the dishes. Getting up from the swing seat, spanking dust from the tail of my apron, I heeded.

"Thought you run away," he said, giving me a look of impatient relief. He was itchy. He told me he had to leave for town, muy pronto, as soon as he could get things straightened up. Motioning me to hand him used dishes one at a time from the accumulation on the kitchen table, he cleared each off and put it in a rack for washing. When I cautiously handed him a gold-rimmed dinner plate containing some drumsticks that still had good meat on them, I was tempted to ask whether I might have them. But before I could make up my mind, Sam dumped the chicken legs in the scrap pan, and taking it outside the screen door, he gave a keen dog-whistle. Two sad-eyed, droop-eared, red-and-tan hounds bounded up and nosed hungrily, but selectively, among the table scraps.

When the dishes were ready for the dishpan, Sam took a quick glance at the stove clock and began shuffling out of his grease-stained apron. His hat fell off in the process, and having become suspicious, I tried to pick it up and see whose initials were branded on the inside hat band, Jules' hat having disappeared about two weeks ago. But Sam beat me to it. He was the quickest man I ever met.

Taking a pencil and pad from a table drawer he said, "Let's see—flour, sugar, baking powder, lard. You think of anything else, Miss Leaf?"

"Toothpicks," I said.

"Gracias, Miss Leaf. You got good memory." He added toothpicks to the list.

He slipped a brown hand through his silver and turquoise bracelet, looked the kitchen over, and gave me parting instructions.

"Miss Bynum say Miss Leaf wash pots, pans, and dishes. Leave dishes on dining table. Miss Bynum put away—they imported. Everything cleaned up, floor swept, you go home. Bye Miss Leaf. Pleased to meecha. Hasta luego."

Raising a hand to the brim of the dove-gray stetson in farewell salute, Sam shut the screen door behind him and whistled for the dogs. I soon heard the spinning wheels of the Flying B's spring wagon on its way to market. I felt lonely.

13

For two solid hours by the stove clock I worked like a beaver, washing and drying all the dishes and silverware, neatly laying them out on the dining table as directed. I scrubbed pots, pans, and kettles until my fingers were sore. I swept up all the trash from the kitchen floor and whooshed it out of the screen door. When I got through with my assigned chores, and some extras for good measure, I flopped on a kitchen chair for a blow.

The aristocratic residence was creepily quiet and seemed sort of scary now. Outside, though, I could hear the distant throb of the threshing machine, and from closer in came the rhythmic scrape of a windmill wheel that could use some grease. At hand, I could hear Pancho Villa meowing at the screen door to get in. The whole outside world seemed to be going on as it should, but inside the big house, all was a tomb.

On tiptoe, I crept to the open door leading to the hall and coughed. Nothing happened.

"I've done my work and I want to go home," I tearfully begged of the emptiness. "How about my fifty cents?" But there was no recognition.

Feeling humbled, beholden to my superiors, unworthy even of four bits, I slipped out of the back door and untied Blackie, who also hadn't eaten. Together we headed down Bynum Road toward the section line where we would turn left.

The tired western sun leaned from its golden chariot to survey the tight rim of the endlessly-sighing prairie for a place to make its bed. I wished to God I could crawl in beside it, close my eyes, and never ever wake up. Never ever.

The emotionally and physically laden pilgrim put the "Incident at the Flying B" back on memory's shelf, along with kindred records relating to a youthful dream of a career with her pen.

At the time of the "incident," she had been a sensitive, immature adolescent with no prior experience to cushion life's hurtful strains. More child than woman, she had returned to her home in profound despair, believing the play to be over, and suffering from such deep humilation over an inadequate performance that she wondered whether she had anything to live for.

As time and life took hands and plodded through the years, however, she came to know that the "Incident at the Flying B" was but a prologue. In the Theater made of Life there are thousands of performances by a multitude of variously equipped human beings—some strong, some weak; some who give while others take; some who build while others destroy; some who feast while others die of starvation. And somewhere along the line there are others who walk ahead questioning.

In the gleam of remembrance's feeble candle, she now read two postscripts to the Incident at the Flying B.

1) In a week or maybe ten days after the incident, Mama received a fifty cent check from Clovis Bynum for the services of her daughter, Leaf Marie, on the 12th inst.

2) Sam Lee was fired as cook for the Flying B when it developed that he was as fast with a marked deck as with a frying pan. Jule went to the depot to see Sam off and he got his stetson back. The parting was amiable. Sam handed him the hat and they shook hands. Sam said he wouldn't need the hat in San Francisco, where he was opening up his own restaurant.

Wondering whatever happened to Sam, she closed the book.

A week or so later, while laboriously coping with a stretch of yucca, sage, and dune, she heard an echoic flourish of steam whistle toots, as if an impatient locomotive engineer was trying to scare a cow off the tracks. She was completely taken aback and a bit shaken, because she was not supposed to be this far north. She scanned the hoop of the mesmerizing plain for a stain of train smoke. Finding none, she began to question the accuracy of her hearing mechanism. But when a couple of All Clear! toots informed that the obstructionist had, indeed, moved out of the way of the cowcatcher, she knew she was within sound range of a real live train.

Like Pavlov's dog, she began to drool. Recollection of that two-hour train ride, the only one she was ever to take, always aroused an almost savage appetite for oranges. By determined effort, reinforced by a couple of cactus apples, she subdued the craving, or rather assigned it to a proper niche in the hall of time.

Blowing the dust off the pertinent chapter, she began to read:

My opportunity to ride a train came about in an unexpected way. Toward the end of my senior year at Prairie View High, I was awarded a tuition-free scholarship to La Flor College. I shall never forget that most unusual day, a day that took me by the shoulders, turned me around almost against my will, and faced me in another direction.

Gossip in the halls, at the cooler, and on the front steps overwhelmingly indicated that Jerome Willis, who could play Melody in F on the piano and who was the teacher's pet, had the scholarship sewed up. So, since I knew I couldn't win, I decided not to take time away from geometry, which I was on verge of flunking, to wordify on the common theme "Youth Today."

On the final day for submissions, Miss Spain, our English teacher, who was in charge of the scholarship program, announced that her room was being set aside from 3:00 until 4:30 to accommodate those who had not yet turned in essays. She emphasized that total participation was expected.

Some half dozen of us laggards dutifully assembled at 3:00 and began scribbling, erasing, and whispering about such a waste of time. Seeing that a note was being passed around, I stared into space in pretended contemplation and let my left hand lower for interception.

It read:

"Jerome's little sister blabbed to Effie Montoya's little sister that Miss Spain helped Jerome with his essay. Why should we waste our time?"

As I passed the note on, I nodded agreement in principle. But since I lived three miles out in the country and I had to get home in time to do the milking, I thought I'd better quit fooling around and turn in something or other so I could go home.

With an assenting nod from Miss Spain, I picked up my Big Chief writing tablet and penny lead pencil and moved away from the others, especially from Buck Yocum, who sat across from me. Living up to his reputation as class clown, he was drawing attention to himself by vocally composing a masterpiece in Igpay Atinlay.

The relatively peaceful desk I chose was near a west window, where I could look out upon the vast, easy unbrokenness of my beloved prairie. With my sharp-nubbed pencil charting the way, I entered a world of my own. What I wrote wouldn't matter, because no one would ever read it anyway. I was seventeen so why not let my hair down?

This I did, setting forth the frustrations a young girl faces in trying to adjust to a rigid society of mixed values, and by the deadline at 4:25 I had got a lot off my chest.

In about a week, maybe ten days, Miss Spain came in one morning with her hair hennaed and wearing a new blue waist with a ruffled bertha. There was a lot of whispering and nodding. We were about to chorus "Happy Birthday" when Mr. Acuff, the principal, came in and with his usual glued-on smile, handed Miss Spain a sealed envelope. When he bowed and left, we knew the letter was from La Flor College and we knew why Miss Spain was all dolled up. Being suspicious of the scholarship deal, as were a lot of my classmates, I figured Miss Spain knew what was in the letter already. But in that I had taken too much for granted. Apparently only knowing that the letter had arrived, she had dressed up in anticipation. Had she known the envelope's content, she probably would have stayed at home sick.

Waving the sealed envelope before the class, and rapping for order, she gushed over the great honor that had come to one of our dear members whose name the envelope held.

All eyes, including mine, were on Jerome Willis, who shrudded his shoulders in a studied indifference that could not disguise the look of self-esteem on his handsome countenance.

When Miss Spain ceremoniously slit the envelope with the gilded dagger opener presented by the school board for ten years of service, the room was so quiet we could hear the paper rip. Removing the letter and reading the message to herself, she bit her lower lip in perplexity. Then, holding the envelope to the light as if something more believable may have been overlooked, and finding nothing, she braced herself to bravely announce:

"Why it's you Leaf! Stand up and let us have a look at you!"

After she had raised both hands twice in upsy-daisy, and Buck had poked me in the ribs, I halfway got up from my seat to acknowledge the sprinkle of applause stimulated by Miss Spain's brisk clapping and Buck's foot-stamping.

"Would you like to say something to the class, Leaf Marie?" Miss Spain invited. "Tell us how it feels to win a coveted prize."

What I said was, "May I be excused?" Without waiting for permission, demerit or not, I left the room—I'd die before I'd let anyone see me cry—unless, of course, I was listening to sad music.

While I was taking my tacky, hand-me-down coat from the hall rack, I overheard Patricia Baldridge—she had a solid gold lavaliere—say, "I'm glad La Flor gave it to her—the Whitfields are so poor."

Then I knew the answer. For philanthrophic reasons, the scholarship had gone to the most improverished member of the class. Embarrassed and beholden, feeling a desperate need to walk and think, I crossed the dirt road and crawled between parallel strands of bobwar to talk to the prairie. As I had done many times before, I told the far-reaching outlay of evenly breathing grass how today, more than ever, I was confused by the lack of societal integrity. On the one hand the poor, the foreign born, the handicapped, those of alien skin, were looked down upon and never asked to parties. On the other hand organized charity, piously awarded the underprivileged, regardless of merit, thus depriving them of an important essential to a prideful existence. I wanted to stand on my own two feet in human dignity without a handout from anybody. I had a lot of Bagby in me, and tomorrow I just might walk into Mr. Acuff's office and tell him where he could put his scholarship.

Then I saw Mama's bonnet bobbing up and down as she came running across the prairie to meet me. I thought Papa had had another stroke, so I ran like the devil until I saw she was waving a piece of paper.

It was a note Mr. Acuff had asked Mr. Rucker, the mailman, to leave in our box.

It simply read: "Dear Leaf, please see me the first thing in the morning."

Wiping tears of happiness from her wide blue eyes, Mama said, "Mr. Rucker told me Mr. Acuff told him when he gave him the note that there never was any doubt in his mind that your essay would win, that it stood head and shoulders above all the rest."

I just stood there like a stick-in-the-mud. All along I had wanted to go to college so bad, so DAMN bad.

We hadn't seen Jule for over two months, maybe six weeks—not since the time he drove over to take Mama and me to a tent show at Melrose where a road company was putting on "Ten Nights in a Bar-room." When the drunkard threw the glass that struck the forehead of his little daughter who had come to try to take him home, Mama cried, "He's killed her! The low down sot has killed her! See the blood!"

Jule put an arm around Mama, assuring her that the little girl wasn't hurt at all, that the blood was only ketchup. Mama shook her head in disbelief until the same little golden-haired girl, in a short dress, was clapped back and she sang to the evil bartender: "Please Don't Sell Pa Any More Rum."

It was not surprising that we hadn't seen much of Jule lately. Now that he was the proud owner of Tuesday's Ironing, he was a busy hombre. Just the same, when he heard I was leaving to go to college September ninth, he sent word by his wrangler that he would come over early that morning and drive me to the flag stop.

I was packed ready and waiting at the gate that cloudless, honey-sun morning. The early September air was so pure that the flat top of Mesa Redondo stood out on the rim of the prairie in detailed clarity. We didn't see the top of the Round Table often, and Grandma used to wonder why it was such a "come and go" thing. It hung out miles away below the Caprock shelf, but when appropriate atmospherics unveiled the turquoise stump, fine weather was presaged and spirits were lifted, as mine were that exciting morning. They were further heightened when, on the dot of eight, a brand-new, yellow-wheeled buggy with a picture of a flatiron on the back of the seat, pulled up at our place.

Mama came out smiling through her tears. "Since my little bird has to fly away from the nest, it's mighty nice she can go in style."

As she spoke she looked longingly, lovingly upon the spanking one-seater. As far back as I could remember, Mama had dreamed of one day owning a well-to-do conveyance. The dream never materialized, but having one in the family at this late stage came pridefully close, closer than she had ever expected.

Leave-takings having the connotation of farewell forever, I was glad this one was quick. Jule hoisted my tacky suitcase onto the rear carry-all and spread the Chimayo seat blanket. A quick embrace, shared tears, and a wave to Daddy—in spite of the stroke he made it to the window but he couldn't wave back—and we were off.

14

The air was crisp and pumpkiny. Lobo, feeling his oats, trotted so fast down the hard dirt road that the wheels of the smart little transport seemed spokeless. Remembering other trips, I asked about Blackie. Jules shook his head, regretfully allowing that the faithful old mare was stove-up and had sort of taken to loco weed.

"Why," he explained, "sometimes the pore old thing walks backwards when she thinks she's going forward—sure sign of a horse being locoed—or a man either, for that matter." On that, I agreed.

As much as I loved Blackie, I was glad she was not in command on this momentous day, for already over my shoulder I could see a blur of black smoke just above the rim of the flapjack plain. I bit my lower lip in nervous apprehension, and Jule sensed it. Looking at his Elgin, he assured there was plenty of time. Just the same, he ruffled the lines and Lobo broke into a lope. Realizing the mettlesome animal was working into a lather, Jule reigned him to a single-foot, a gait the rambunctious young horse really executed with love. I couldn't help but wonder, though, and I think it crossed Jule's mind, too, how Lobo was going to take it when a steam-snorting rival appeared on the scene.

Although the smoke had not come to a head, and we could still not hear a train sound, I was edgy just the same, being inwardly perturbed over the giant step I was taking away from my own little world into a world I knew not of.

Whether Jule sensed my mood or not, he began to sing an old square dance ditty we used to stomp to at Tarpley's barn. I joined in:

> Oh, there once was a miller boy
> That lived by the mill
> If he ain't moved away
> He's livin' there still.
>
> Oh, the mill wheel turned
> Of it's own free will
> If the creek still runs
> It's a turnin' still.
>
> Hand on the hopper

Foot on the slack
Turn around
And go right back!

Jule offered me his arm to promenade the turn, and we both laughed like anything. But as we both knew we must, we returned to silent thought. I was about to tell him I would miss our old times together, but the face I looked upon was a much older one than I had known, and was immersed in deep thought, as if something was weighing on his mind. I elected to keep quiet.

In the meantime, the fetching carriage surmounted the shining parallel tracks at the whistle stop, and Jule slued to bring Lobo to a whoa behind a dense stand of gray-berried juniper.

"Wait, Hon," he said, as I knew he would, for in maturity my dear uncle had become gentlemanized. Why, with his background, I never knew. In his youth—he was twenty eight now—he had gotten into all manner of scrapes with fellow rowdies, but as a man he turned a leaf. He never asked a girl to dance with him without first putting his coat on, and he never, ever butted a girl while dancing. In fact, the girls often said that waltzing with Jule was as relaxing as rocking in an old porch rocker. Oh, he still got in a fight once in a while, but only to protect his honor. But he never carried brass knucks, even though he easily could have, because Grandpa's hung on a nail over the washstand. And he never, ever, shot a rabbit or a prairie dog with a pistol. No gentleman would ever do that.

In ladylike dignity, I waited while he unhooked the traces and tied Lobo to a sturdy off-side branch of a juniper, where he would not have to face what was coming up. Then my uncle gave me his hand, assisting me to alight as a proper young lady should. With the rainbow-rayed Chimayo blanket across an arm and my shabby, rope-tied suitcase in his free hand, he led the way to the flag stop.

Depositing the articles at the cross buck, looking at his Elgin, and sighting down the still clear track, he spoke, "The time has come, Hon."

"Yes," I said, for I had been waiting for it.

"Opal and me got hitched in Tucumcari last Monday. We haven't broke the news to her folks or mine yet, but I just couldn't let you go away without knowin'."

We embraced and he wiped a tear from my eyes with his bandana. "I'm so glad," I told him. "Mama will be, too. Break the good news to her on your way back. Now tell me all about it."

With a cautious eye on the oncoming plume, he began telling about it, and fast.

"Last Monday I went to "Tucum" to get my hail insurance straightened out, and I stopped by the Antlers for a cup of Java. And guess who sashayed up to take my order, looking all blue-eyed, blond and pretty as a picture? I had already heard she had give that old polecat his walking papers, and it didn't make me a bit mad. He never had any intention of marrying her. He was just out for a good time. Well, the other waitress took the customers, and Opal sat down and had a cup with me. She was mighty blue as she told me all about it. Seems a fellow came in from Oklahoma and she served him hot cakes and they got to talkin'. He said he had come there lookin' for his brother-in-law, Speed Turley, a broomcorn buyer. He said his sister was sick, and he was bringin' Speed a message from her.

"I know a Speed Turley," Opal says to this man. "But he's a single man."

"And this Oklahoma man, he was from Guthrie, took a picture out of his wallet and said, "Is this the man you know?"

She looked at the snapshot of a family in front of a nice white frame house. The man had his arm around a nice looking little woman, and two young'uns were on tricycles in front of them. "By God, that's Speed all right!" she said to the Oklahoma man.

"And she told me that honest to Pete, she was so humiliated, hurt, and mad that she wanted to puke. But being on the job, she tried not to show it. The Oklahoma man saw through her, though, and told her he was sorry he got her so upset. Then he put the picture back in his wallet, paid the check, and left.

"Well, she told me she boiled all afternoon, but kept on at work. About four o'clock, she looked out of the winder and saw Speed's buggy come spinnin' down main street. She took her apron off and went to meet him. She called on him whether he had courted her under the false pretense that he was single, and he had to own up. Quite a crowd gathered, and she blessed him out right there before God and everybody, including his brother-in-law. She told him if he ever darkened her door again he'd be met by the business end of her Daddy's fortyfour. Speed's brother-in-law got in the buggy with him and they left town."

Jule sighted down the track. "Well, Hon, to make a long story short I didn't fool around. I took her by the hand like I should of done years ago and led her right over to the court house before they closed, and got her hitched to me for life."

A shrill flourish of monosyllabic toots punctuated the ripe autumn air. Panic-stricken, Lobo reared on his hind legs, neighing with obscene flared lips exposing angry rows of square, yellow horse teeth.

"Well, here she comes! I hope to God Lobo don't break loose and charge the damn thing when it makes its stop. I paid two hundred dollars for him," Jules remarked as he swung the Chimayo blanket high in the air.

A stutter of succinct blasts acknowledged the flag, brakes hacked and coughed, and Jules bestowed a quick kiss upon my forehead as he handed over the valise and hurried to the rapidly fragmenting juniper.

This being the first train I ever caught, I was touched by the contagion of Lobo's panic. Although the denim arm of the man at the throttle signaled, "stop," leading me to believe the train would halt at my side, it did no such thing. The inclined frame of the cowcatcher kept plowing ahead of the fractious engine that was splattering sharp, stinking cinders and spewing squirts of hot steam.

Feeling deserted, like Lobo I wanted to break away from this iron monster and gallop back to the safety of the home corral. Then came a reassuring screech of brakes and a slowdown that steadied my nerves a bit, and through the windows of the freshly painted yellow coaches I looked upon relaxed, idly concerned faces of seasoned travelers. I felt silly. There was nothing to be afraid of. Not really.

A metallic shudder rumbled along the couplings from the tender right down to the mail car. With a sudden jerk, the train hesitated on its tracks. At my very side, a door opened and a uniformed trainman stepped down with a little stool in his hand. Placing it on the ground, he beckoned and called "All aboard!"

Now that the train hadn't gone off and left me all alone standing there by the tracks, I knew how to act, for I had seen self-confident people, some as rural as I, calmly get on and off trains at the depot at Melrose.

"La Flor," I announced as I and my shabby valise were hoisted to a trembling little floor over the coupling.

"Vamonos!" the conductor called, waving the train on and swinging up.

Picking up what must have been the tackiest piece of luggage on earth, he led me into the coach and directed me to an unoccupied seat where I kerflopped.

Warning me to mind my head, he hefted my shoddy canvas valise onto an overhead framework, edging it into sorry alignment with stylish grips and suitcases of genuine cowhide, and one that looked like real 'gator.

"Fare?"

Embarrassed for having allowed myself to be dunned, I unknotted my handkerchief and counted out six bits. With bold, scientific interest, I watched the conductor assign the coins to their appropriate slots in a shiny, metal doodad hitched to his belt. Having lived on a dryland farm all my life, and being well acquainted with all manner of tools and instruments, some through personal use, others from observations in store windows and catalogs, I could comprehend the practicality of the neat cash belt. Utterly mystifying, though, was the little punched card the conductor slipped edgewise under a small, metal cleat attached to the polished mahogany window frame at my side, just above my head. I was tempted to ask him what I was supposed to do with the card, but I restrained myself fearing the gesture would only further accent my rurality.

During a swerve of the tracks, I swayed toward the window and caught a glimpse of Jule, Lobo, and the yellow-wheeled buggy going home to a well-deserved good life. By scratching his fingers to the bone and with a little help from Grandpa's will, he had been able to piece enough money together to put a down payment on the goal of his ambition—Tuesday's Ironing. With his lost love back into his life, he was doubly blessed. They never should have split up in the first place.

I knew it wasn't Christian to blame the dead, especially relatives, but I always thought, and Mama did, too, that Granny's everlasting to-do over Opal's Mama being a mail order bride started it all. Opal had just got damn sick and tired of the gossip that was making the rounds, and she had thrown Jule over for that broomcorn buyer who didn't have any more morals than a tomcat. Jule had taken it mighty hard. Mighty hard.

For my part, even as a little young'un, I had thought it was nobody's business if Myrt had gotten off the train at Melrose wearing a slit skirt that showed a black lace garter. She was in good health, and Jimsam liked what he got. The important thing was they got along, and they dearly loved their daughter. If Myrt wasn't any prize, neither was Jimsam. Why Myrt had once confided to Mama that it took her five years to break Jimsam from calling a handkerchief a snot rag.

Sitting there on the soft, hairy green seat, I yawned. I had gotten up at five to tote fodder and do the milking, because the boy Jule was sending over to help Mama couldn't get there until this evening. My shoulders were so slouchy-tired I started to slump, but although the assumed posture was one of strained dignity, I straightened up and remained so, because I was going away to college.

Presently, the clacking, throbbing train for some fool reason got stuck in its tracks, and the peaceful western landscape trundled past my window in complete indifference to the train's plight. A cowboy at the crossroads high-signed "Howdy-Adios."

Lavendar-gray mesas, indifferently grazing white-face cattle, an octagonal, windowless hogan with a wisp of smoke rising from the center vent, some white goats and one black one, a busy windmill, all slipped quietly past, as if conforming to a regular schedule, while the train just sat there and shook. Strangely enough no one else in the coach was aware of the train's predicament. Not wanting to make a fool of myself, I shut my eyes to the moving landscape and leaned back in my seat, assigning the phenomenon to the illusory family of mirage, aurora, and something about angular vision that my geometry teacher could never get through my kind of head.

When I finally opened my eyes, the situation had reversed. Now the train and I were moving ahead while the landscape stayed put. I felt embarrassed for having been tooken, and I was glad I hadn't tried to get fellow passengers to get off with me and help pry the train loose.

The terrain now was level, and the little train got down to business. The monotonous articulation of the wheels disposed passengers to fall into personal molds. Down the aisle, a few seats to the left, a ranch couple on the way to the bedside of a dying mother had put down their basket of home-grown valley apples that they invited fellow passengers to share along with their sad story—the call had come at two in the morning. Now, leaning against each other, they catnapped. Across the aisle, a leather-faced cowhand who was a little drunk fell asleep sitting straight up. The elderly, bearded gentleman across the aisle, one seat removed, settled more deeply in the book he was reading.

Influenced by the easy attitudes of the others in the coach, I leaned back and began to nod, only to discover that the atmosphere of group relaxation did not extend to the seat back of mine, where a pair of young roughnecks were feeling their oats.

Slapping their thighs to keep time, the licquored-up rousters began to sing:

Oh, the funniest sight I ever seen
Was when the tomcat jumped on the sewing machine.
Oh, the sewing machine went so fast
It sewed ninety-nine stitches up the tomcat's . . . foot.

The conductor, who was sitting at the far end of the coach making out a report, put his papers in his pocket and came down the aisle. "Now, you boys keep quiet!" he warned. As soon as he left the coach, the lads engaged in some muffled, slubby talk of an ungentlemanly nature, keeping their voices toned down so I, alone, could hear. Pretty soon they began badgering each other as to who should make the first move. Embarrassed, I ignored the whiskied youths, feeling that having nothing else to do, they were undertaking a fishing expedition, and when I didn't rise to the bait, they would calm down. So I sat perfectly still looking out of my window, paying them no notice at all. This apparently only egged them on. Pretty soon one of them challenged the other. "I'll bet you five, you ain't got the Goddamn nerve."

"Hell, give me another snort and I'll take you up," the second one boasted. "I'm gonna make her turn around and when she does, I'll cast a sheep's eye, and I'll be sittin' with her holdin' her hand and when we go through the tunnel, I'll git myself somethin' mighty sweet."

With that, a suggestive knee-nudge pressed against the back of my seat, making free with the vicinity of my lower spine. In angry humiliation, that anybody should take me for that kind of girl, I thought of asking the elderly couple in the seat ahead to change places with me, but when I saw they both were snoozing, I removed to the opposite end of my green hair cushion. A hinged knee nudged again.

Enough was enough! Avoiding the eyes of the tipsy rowdies, I looked the coach over for a vacant seat. Finding none, I decided to move to the rear and stand near the cooler. With this some of the passengers turned in their seats and looked in the direction of the bottle-happy hellions.

"Whur's the conductor?" somebody asked.

With that the elderly gentleman with an open book on his lap raised his graying head and peered over his gold-rimmed spectacles to assess a situation that had just come to his attention. Then, closing his book, he arose to an erect physical stature untouched by the hand of time, smiled warmly, and extended a hand.

"May I introduce myself? I am Giles Baugh of La Flor College. And you must be the incredible young lady called Leaf, whose essay won our scholarship. I suspected you might be on this train, but as usual I lost myself between the covers of my book."

Overwhelmed by the reverse flow of the tide, I could only accept his hand, albeit weakly, and nod. To risk a word was to risk a tear.

He understood. "Dear Lady, may I have the honor of being your seatmate?"

"Please do," I managed to say. I resumed my seat and made room for him at my side.

Reaching back for his little punched card, he slipped it into the slot with mine, and my heart went pitty-pat.

15

While the determined little train happily pursued its track across desert and plain, Dr. Baugh told me how highly he regarded my remarkable essay on "Youth Today," and how after reading it all other entries paled.

This being the first official praise ever bestowed upon me, and because of a certain native reticence—Mama and Daddy used to worry because sometimes I used to crawl under the bed and refuse to come out until company left—I just sat there like a lump on a log, mute and goose-pimply, unable to express my feelings that curiously concerned the proximity of an attractive older man with only the hyphen of his book between our thighs.

He tried to draw me out with questions about my home and family, my likes and dislikes, the kinds of books I liked to read. After a while my perfunctory answers apparently made him decide to let me thaw out. In the meantime, I sat in awkward silence, watching the easy unroll of high plains, yucca, stock grass, and not much else except distance. Pretty soon the lonely, skeletal framework of an old wooden windmill tower, just like the one at home, stood out against the cloudless, azure sky.

Dr. Baugh spoke. "A solitary windmill standing by itself on the vast prairie is the epitome of loneliness."

Then, as if seeing me for the first time, he eyed me with a twinkle of surprise, "My dear girl, you smiled—a sly, little smile of doubt. Don't you agree?"

The cat let go of my tongue. "Yes, Sir, I agree to a certain extent. An old wooden windmill tower standing all alone with nothing man-made like a shanty or a corral to keep it company does have a lonesome look. But it's New Mexico—desolate, lonely, and lovely. And home."

He patted my hand in sympathetic understanding. "I was born and reared in Maine a long, long time ago, but my eyes still mist when I recall the pines of Bowdoin. Even though a couple of years as a rancher of sorts restored my health, for which I have been eternally grateful, at heart I still am a New Englander, a yankee. And if I read you correctly, you always will be una Nueva Mejicana."

"Si, Senor," I replied in kindred, unmusical accent that surely neither of us would have exposed to native Spanish ears.

This bit of ice-breaking over, he spoke freely about his plans for me at La Flor, repeating what Mr. Acuff already had explained. La Flor was not abundantly endowed. Its scholarships provided tuition and books only. In my case, nevertheless, food, lodging, and a personal allowance would be provided in exchange for my assistance in the kitchen, dining room, and laundry—a welcome procedure that heightened my desire to stand on my own two feet.

Presently, I became aware of the strangest thing coming down the aisle—a man wearing a store! Approaching us was a slight, sallow-complexioned youth in a railroad uniform of dark blue serge with sleeve cuffs edged in gold braid. An aisle-wide, polished wooden tray bearing folded newspapers, assorted fruits, candies, chewing wax, and cigars, swung from a long leather strap encircling the seller's neck, leaving his hands free to hand out purchases and make change. Men delved into pockets for coins, craning their necks to see what they would buy.

I was attracted to the hands of the news butch—that's what I heard somebody say he was. They were paler and softer than any hands I had ever seen. They were beautiful. I supposed he must be from the city. How wonderful, I thought, to have a job where the wind, the cold, the hard labor never toughened one's hands. Even at almost eighteen, my paws were as rough as whet leather. And I was a girl.

Half-rising, Dr. Baugh, as if in regular procedure, dropped a coin in a tin cup and picked up a copy of the Rocky Mountain Sun. His main attention was on something else though, something he was appraising with the eye of a man of experience. Turning to me, he said, "May I buy you an orange?"

I knew that no subsequent human utterance could have outweighed the sweetness of his words. His baggy tweed suit became shining armor.

"Thank you, Sir, I'd love an orange."

When my eager eyes focused upon two expensive oranges, half again as big as any I had ever seen, each poised in a gay tissue boat, my gastric juices began to pour. Imagine having an orange, except at Christmas! I craved to rip off the rinds and gobble up. But remembering that I no longer was a country young'un but a young lady in the company of a distinguished gentleman, I knew I must await proper presentation. The ritual of preparation was wonderous to behold, and well worth the wait.

My benefactor took a white linen handkerchief from his pocket and spreading it across his knees, he laid the fruits upon it. Then, carefully selecting the more perfectly contoured of the yellow spheres that I knew must be for me, he unhitched a delicate, pearl-handled penknife from his watch fob, and plunged the bold little blade into the navel axis of my orange, releasing tantalizing sub-acid aroma that set my mouth watering more than ever. Hungrily, I watched the rind being marked off from pole to pole. By loosening and pressing each section of rind down, Dr. Baugh's genius converted my orange into an exotic, white-petaled flower. Still in its tissue boat, the masterpiece changed hands.

By this time Dr. Baugh was hungry, too, and the two of us lost no time in devouring the treat. Then he wiped my fingers on a corner of his handkerchief.

Assembling the orange peelings and the well-sucked residue of lith, wrapping the waste in the limp tissue boats, Dr. Baugh excused himself to take it to a flip-lidded can under the water cooler at the far end of the coach.

In the meantime a lean, beet-faced man whose sunburnt hair was the color of binder twine paused at my side, steadying his spare, shoddily garbed frame by hanging onto the metal handhold of my seat.

It was Clement Scarfield. I had not seen him for several years, years that Mama said were of good riddance, for Clem was known as a ne'er do well. He and

Jule had gotten into a lot of devilment when young sprouts, but Jule had straightened out. Grandpa saw to it that he did. But no Pa was around with a strap to show Clem the straight and narrow. So he kept on getting into and out of scrapes, never could get much of a job or hold one after he got it. Just the same, Clem was a friendly, likeable cuss, and rather good-looking when young. But you'd never know it to see him now.

When he got that little schoolmarm over at Buckwheat in a family way and she had to go back to Texas—at least that's what everybody said—Jule, upon Grandpa's admonition, began avoiding Clem. The break didn't come, though, until they accidentally rode onto each other while hunting strays.

Jule said they were just riding along, smoking and chewing the fat, when a little old prairie dog stood upon his mound and yakked at Clem. Clem said, "I've been barked at all my life, but when the prairie dogs take it up, that's the end." He pulled his pistol out and shot the prairie dog dead.

Jule spurred and rode off in the opposite direction. He told Mama that maybe it wouldn't have looked so bad if Clem hadn't killed the prairie dog with a pistol.

I was in a nervous fidget. Scarfield was hanging on, looking me over, trying to place me, although the conductor had motioned him to move on. I sure didn't want him to be there when my important new friend came back. Whether the good man sensed my awkward position, I shall never know. On his way back to our seat, he paused to shake hands and chat with the saddened couple who were on the deathbed mission, and they offered him apples.

"Young Lady, didn't I see Old Jule Bagby at the stop whur you got on?" Clem said. "You kinfolk to him?"

"Yes, Sir," I said.

With his head leaned so close I could smell his antidote, he said, "Young Lady, I've been lookin' at you, and I think I used to know you. Ain't you the little gal Jule used to take to Sunday school—Frank and Ethel Whitfield's girl?"

When I admitted my identity, I heard one of the boys in the seat back of mine—I had forgotten all about them—say to the other, "Take his quarter and go see if the butch has got any sen sen."

"My, how time flies!" Scarfield commented. "How old are you now?"

I didn't have to answer because someone had to get by. Clem pulled in what little he had to pull in and asked a new question.

"What's Old Jule doin' now?" His tone implied he supposed Jule wasn't doin' much of anything. "He still goin' with one of the Ginster girls?"

I shrugged, letting my indifference infer that Jule's business was none of mine or anybody else's. Clem sure was behind the times, what with being away for some four or five years while something or other he was mixed up in blowed over.

"What do you hear from Old Cooter? Him and me had a lot of fun together."

"Mama had a card from him the other day. He was in Trinidad."

"What's Old Cooter doin' in Coloraydo? I thought he joined the navy?"

"Seems there's another Trinidad in the Caribbean Sea, off the coast of South America some place," I explained.

"I'll be damned. Live and learn," Clem declared.

A man in uniform—I hadn't seen him before—came up and said, "Come with me Scarfield," motioning Clem to walk ahead.

As I watched him go, I felt a surge of compassion for Clem. His daddy had run off and left his mama and him and his little sister. Miz Scarfield was a good woman.

She took in washing that Clem picked up and delivered. When she died, the young'uns were handed from relative to relative until they were old enough to run away.

Unwelcoming him seemed right at the time and place, but now I felt bereft and contrite. I wondered for what damn purpose, for whose damn good a human creature was thrown without choice into a world where his very existence had to be bought by connivance and humiliation, even crime? There must be, there had to be an answer some place. Sure was something to think about.

Dr. Baugh shook hands again with the low-spirited couple and resumed his place at my side. He offered me first look at his newspaper, but for once I had no interest in the Katzenjammer Kids. I shook my head, and while he read, I stared across the ever-changing, ecru plain, interrupted here and there by a raw arroyo, a stand of yellowing cottonwoods, or a distant tetilla.

The steam whistle uncapped a lonesome "Whoooeee—whooeee," and over our heads two rangy bodies, with grimy shirttails riding above silver-buckled, rattlesnake belts exposing naked belly hairs, reached tall to bring down a couple of rawhide valises. The impatient train jerked to a halt, and the boys, redolent of sen sen, the sure thing for whiskey breath, paused single file at my side, each politely touching his roll brim stetson.

"For you Ma'am," the taller said as his free hand placed in my lap a wrapped candy box with a pretty red bow on top. "The butch was out of horehound."

Startled at realizing these boys were Aunt Noonie's two sons, I could only say "Thank you."

The boys swung off at a flag stop as overgrown with desolation as the one where I had boarded. As the train moved, Dr. Baugh and I exchanged waves of "adios" with them. Alf and Nim were their names I remembered. The last we saw of them they were hoofing it down the road toward the wooden windmill scaffolding, a cedar post corral and a lonely unpainted shanty.

"Ornery cusses," Dr. Baugh said. "But as honest and hard-working boys as the day is long. I've known them since they were in knee pants."

"And so have I," I muttered, but he did not hear.

"I'm glad they made a gesture of apology to you," he continued. "They were just whiskied up. Life has been pretty dull for them since their mother remarried and moved back to Arkansas."

I already knew Uncle Nimrod, Grandpa's younger brother, had died in the pen, but Aunt Noonie's remarriage was real news. Maybe I could get a line off to Mama tonight, for I sure had a lot to tell.

The steam whistle called again, and Dr. Baugh folded his copy of the Rocky Mountain Sun and slipped it into a side pocket of his jacket.

"La Flor is the next stop. I'd better look after our luggage."

When he saw my fingers working at the red bow on the candy box, he scolded, "Not yet, Little Girl! Supper will be waiting for us."

Thus ended the narration of the scholarship and train ride, the only train ride she ever would take. For many years this final chapter of her youthful autobiography laid mute and faded in a ribbon-tied bundle in Mama's old trunk. After the funeral the papers took up other residence, and as if foreknowing they'd be carried away as millet seeds on the winds of time, they had indelibly imprinted themselves on the enduring tablet of her memory.

It was not surprising that this was her last literary effort. In addition to her homework, the kitchen and dining room duties at La Flor College, left precious little time for diarizing. Besides, thinking and dreaming on paper was out of phase with a maturing appreciation of writing of a distinctive quality. The list Dr. Baugh assigned to her to read was long, long and wonderful. Through the courtesy of a lamp at her cot, she read far into the night.

The more she sampled the good bread of classical literature, the more she realized her own inadequacy. Granted, she may have inherited something of her father's love of the literary arts, but she was also the daughter of a practical mother, who didn't know B from Bull's Foot about Shakespeare, but sure knew how to stretch a dime.

Upon learning that Milton got less that fifteen dollars for *Paradise Lost*—not enough to buy a good calf—that Sam Butler, her very favorite, didn't live to realize one red cent for *The Way of All Flesh*, and that E. A. Poe didn't get enough for *The Raven* to buy a bag of bird feed, she decided there wasn't much future in the writing business.

Just the same, the writing itch was not something you could not cure with a dab of Mother Brown's salve, so she continued to piddle around with it for awhile, sending letters on human rights to the Tucumcari Star. They actually published a couple of them before she had to give up because of lack of stamp money.

The lowering sun placed the wayfarer on location, and it was about time. The trouble with getting all tangled up with memorabilia was that it was bad for one's presence of mind. Take the time she had gotten all teared-up over an old love affair, and not seeing where she was going, she had stepped in a gopher hole and turned an ankle—the left one that time.

Adjusting her burden and lengthening her stride to make up for time lost while strolling memory's lane, she wondered what the Sam Hill it had been that had sent her human soul with pick and spade into the ancient mounds of the past.

Oh, Yes! It was the cautious "toot-toot" of a locomotive. If that's what it was and she hoped it wasn't—it would have had to come from the Chili Line, and she wanted no further part of it. The coldest she ever was in her life was while loading wool at Buckman, and she still had her coat then. Best forget it.

Steadily, wearily, she walked onward into the saffron glow of eventide, pausing only to take nourishment from an open-air market of maroon cactus apples. As is often the case in life, especially in regard to seed catalogues, the display proved more palatable to the eye than the fruit to the tooth. The mouthwatering ripe tunas she took were cram full of seeds. She managed to bite into quite a few just the same, always mindful to expectorate the seeds for other animals who would consume and pass them, thus maintaining bionomic balance of the land. Actually, she must have swallowed more prickly pear seeds than she thought, because before long she began to feel bloated. Feeling no better fast, she spread her bed between convenient yucca steeples. She did not lie down immediately, though. According to the family doctor book, a person with bloated innards wasn't supposed to. So she just sat and squirmed.

Her indisposition brought to mind the time Grover Cleveland and Benjamin Harrison got into the turnip patch after a rain. Relief came to them through a prostrate revolving and trumpeting therapy that the men found highly amusing, but didn't want the woman to watch.

Although she, herself, enjoyed warm rapport with those good-natured products of a mare and a donkey—and her intrinsic stubbornness often had been thus likened—she was not about to lie down and roll. Instead, she sat cross-legs on the Two Grey Hills with extremities decently covered, and after several uks, things calmed down, and she was able to sleep.

The next morning she was combed and fed and on her way ahead of an oversleeping sun. The eastern sky was an archipelago of little cottonball clouds that pinked before her eyes, and then deepened to rose for one glorious moment before being neutralized by the emerging day star.

Through the combined hospitalities of weather and terrain, she made good time for the next four or five days. Her way was even bettered by a feeling of a personal nature, like maybe she knew ahead of time what she would find around the next bend. So she was not at all surprised one evening when she walked up to a stout company of Spanish bayonets guarding a well-groomed campsite. The surprise came the next morning when she woke up.

"La Mesita!" she cried in startled disbelief. "Dadgummit, why didn't somebody tell me?"

In two shakes, she was hurrying as fast as her hastily packed burden would allow in the direction of La Flor.

16

She hurried as fast as she could, but when she paused to blow, there was no trace of La Flor. All she could see was a stand of yellowing old trees and some kind of sagging wooden scaffold.

Knowing something was out of kilter, but not knowing what, she halted before approaching the trees and cautiously called out, "You all have been around here for considerable time. Ever hear of a place called La Flor?"

A responding rustle of breeze and falling leaves revealed a decrepit, topless old windmill tower, and beyond it a community of fallen walls. The old Dempster that she had known so well was on its last legs, but it had held up long enough to tell the tale. La Flor del Llano was gone. "non est" as her Latin teacher used to say for "It ain't no more."

In its day, this proud bonneted scaffold had supplied water for the whole town, the college, the depot, the businesses, livestock, and all. Unbelievably, a rickety, headless skeleton, some moribund elms, and the rubble of fallen walls were all that was left now. All except remembrance of how it was. Memory took over and led the way.

She knew it was a Monday, that day so long ago, because with a galvanized bucket in each hand she came to this very spot to get wash water. Being the youngest and strongest of the girls who were working for room and board, she had been chosen water bearer for the laundry shed on wash day. (For years afterwards she blamed the stretch imposed by this exercise, that came to include providing water for the dormitory kitchen and dining room as well, for the embarrassing length of her arms, preferring to carry a clutch purse under an arm rather than a handled one that would hang below her knees. Later on, of course, she realized that long arms were a natural heritage, and she not only was unashamed of them, but there were times they came in mighty darn handy, like in pitching hay.)

On that radiant spring Monday so long ago, the graveled path leading from the college buildings to the town's water source, a chipper new windmill, had been prettified by a border of spring flowers. Then was the season of two of her favorites, cupped crocuses of Guadalupe blue, and prim, butter-bonneted jonquils. Shielding the flower beds from the path's commerce was an edging of sized and snugged crystal specimens got from a nearby mine. She loved the flowers and the quartz and often she would let her pails overfill at the spurting lead pipe so that on her way back she could slosh some water to slake the thirst of the flowers and at the same time wash dust off the surfaces of the precious ore specimens.

It was during this gesture of mingled admiration and good will that she saw the men coming. She and her buckets moved out of the way of the approaching, white-uniformed Woodmen of the World each, but one, carrying a spade over his shoulder.

By that time, she had been living in the town for over a year, and she knew all the lodge members, at least by sight, for they were established local townsmen. She recognized Mr. Apodaca, the postmaster, Mr. Crabtree, president of the bank, Big Elmer Adler, owner of the livery stable and editor of La Flor Weekly Press, Little Elmer, the college cook, Mr. Grantham, the druggist—he had asthma and did not carry a spade—and Molly Morehouse's husband, Jake, who was a drinking man. On this occasion, though you'd never suspect it, for as he fell into disciplined quickstep as leader of the group, he was all shaved, shorn, and handsome—mighty handsome.

As she watched the men march by, her girlish heart knew the answer to a question often asked in the village—"Why does Molly, who has to make the living, put up with that scalawag?" Molly loved the scalawag.

By this time practically everybody in town, including the teachers and the student body of the college, had assembled at the windmill or were hurrying to get there. She put her buckets down well out of the way and moved in close, but not too close, not being pushy like some people.

Everybody except the dogs stood in head-bowed silence through Big Elmer's invocation, although few understood what he was saying. B.E., as he was known about town, had never had much of a voice, and the prevailing southwest wind in New Mexico was never any good to pray against.

The words of ritual the lodgemen reverently employed were clearly audible, but she did not comprehend their meaning. Nor did she try to. In that day, the word lodge bore a connotation of respected secrecy. If a man got up from the supper table and said he was going to a lodge meeting, eyebrows may have been raised, but no questions were asked.

According to an observing history professor who stood nearby the ritual in progress sprang from the ancient Druids, whoever they were. She had never gotten around to looking them up. When these goings-on were over, all eyes focused on a wet tow sack binding a bundle of treelets. She knew the formalities were related to forestry and were unquestionably noble, high motivation being a natural attribute of any undertaking related to tree culture, open or secret.

The Woodmen took turns spading out holes around the south side of the earthen water tank, except Mr. Grantham, who couldn't do heavy work. He stood aside, resting an arm on a leg of the windmill tower, giving directions about how the work should be done. When the holes were readied to his approval, his moment of action came. He freed the little elmlets from the damp gunny sacking, and tenderly, lovingly set an infant tree in each depression, giving succor to the roots with something smelly shaken from a can.

The ceremony over, the crowd dispersed, and she hurried back to her buckets of water, wondering whether the puny-looking treelets would survive. Upon her next tote, she was more dubious than ever, for they were as bowed as horseshoes. A man in a tan uniform, a man she had never seen before, was standing there looking at the little trees. When he saw her, he tipped his wide-brimmed tan hat. Sensing her doubt, he spoke.

"They'll make it, Young Lady, make it and continue to make it after all else is gone. Chinese elms are like that. But they shouldn't have been planted so close together."

She never did find out who the man was, but he sure knew what he was talking about. Wonder what ever became of him?

But she must hurry. As she moved along, she looked upon the sad, sepulchral remains of the Flower of the Plains where she and many other New Mexicans had acquired at least a nodding acquaintance with acculturation, a step down the road of learning that otherwise never would have been trod, and she felt weak and sick. Gone was the strength, the sinew, everything. Buried in yesterdays' debris was the sum total of a living, breathing community of enlightenment.

Gone was the petty barrier of crossties put up to shield the territorial colonial residence of the town councilman from the unpalatable proximity of Molly Morehouse's ramshackle Lone Star Inn. The spite fence had fallen both ways to lie in silent reconciliation. The collapsed walls of the livery stable where Molly's husband drove when sober enough now were no less prestigious than those of La Flor City Bank.

The caved-in foundations of the Weekly Press reposed beneath a clutter of decaying timbers. When she turned over an old board so she could get by, its faded message still proclaimed THE FASTEST GROWING NEWSPAPER IN NEW MEXICO. Heart-touched, she stood in a moment of reverence in the presence of the residium of the once sprightly little paper that had opened a long sealed family door, revealing, not a nude body of an elderly woman hanging from a rafter by a strip of torn bed sheet, but an undaunted artist sitting at her easel.

It must have been about midway of her second year at La Flor when one morning one of the teachers had left a copy of the weekly on the dining table. While she was clearing the table, her startled eyes focused on an illustrated front page item stating that a New York art dealer had bought GRASSHOPPER IN GOGGLES, a painting by the late Petunia Stoner. The reproduction showed a ripening wheatfield bowing under the pressure of a raging, sand-laden windstorm. In the right hand corner of the turbulent landscape, a large grasshopper wearing heavily-rimmed dust goggles and with a neat white napkin tucked under his chin, munched unperturbedly on a fat ear of wheat.

Although she had never known Aunt Pet, the family bugbear who had been committed to a mental institution where she hanged herself, this star-crossed woman often was in her thoughts. Even as a child, she had always felt a secret curiosity and compassion for her. And looking again at the front page of the La Flor Weekly Press, although hastily, because Mr. Osborne had come back for it, her human self was pervaded by a remorseful but noble melancholy—sad, triumphant, and peculiar. This feeling about Aunt Pet never died. It lived on and on in something Dr. Baugh once said, whether in inspiration, paraphrase, or quote:

"Best not come whole into a fractured world to be broken into conformity."

The memory of Aunt Pet's strange-wayed life drew a veil about itself when an old street sign looked up from a weed bed, reminding her that she was on Lew Wallace Avenue. But where was the gracefully arched depot where her only train ride had terminated? She saw nothing readable in its rubble.

Then the voice of remembrance interposed. "Look."

There appeared a leafed and branched apricot tree, shading a bench where two persons sat—had sat, for it was empty. The apricot tree metamorphosed into the totality of La Flor College, beckoning her to come and read the way it had been. She moved toward a stone-crested jumble that properly had been the last to surrender—the stubborn entranceway of the main building. Even before she left the school—and not entirely of her own accord—this handsome archway had been profaned by the purple paint brush, the signature of a most strange sect that had taken over the bankrupt institution upon Dr. Baugh's death. Traces of the contentious dye still held on segments of the fallen keystone, and she looked down upon it with mixed emotions, for neither side had survived the assessments imposed by time and circumstances.

To her complete surprise, a gatekeeper occupied the surface of a stone fallen from the arch. She spoke to the incredibly beautiful mountain boomer, who remained unmoved on his private observation deck, his beady head resting between under-size forearms, his heavy tail curved in a posture of indifference. While the lizard did not reply, the curtain of time rolled back, and someone else spoke a greeting.

Virgil McIntosh, handsome student-janitor, son of a sheep rancher, opened the great, paneled front door. Taking the burden from her shoulders, resting it at the entranceway, he ushered her into the reception hall, past the mirrored, mahogany hall tree and the venerable grandfather clock with a carved base and an elegantly bonneted top.

Turning left, she entered the cameo-papered dining room, where long pine tables were flanked by long pine benches. She was on her way to the kitchen where she used to lay the next morning's fire in the wood range where, when her day's chores were done, she used to lay on her cot in an adjoining cubicle that once had been a pantry and read by lamplight until sleep came. She was looking for old friends, girls who had worked in the kitchen, too.

Then a hollow, unpersoned voice asked, "Who are you, Girl? What do you want?" And she again found herself looking upon the silent residium of the Flower of the Plains, knowing that in a nostalgic moment she had begged of Providence more than it could give. In trying to find the "used-to-be" she had been confronted by the "is" wearing a different face.

Memory offered a hand, however, and led her back, far back, across hills and valleys of time to a certain garden of realities where she and her benefactor walked, rested, and talked. It was his last summer, although neither of them knew it. It was right over there where they rested—he tired easily—on a wooden bench in the shade of the apricot tree he, himself, had planted. Probing the overhanging, green branches with his cane, he remarked, "Bishop Lamy loved them, too."

Then, as if addressing a class, the old professor declared:

"An infrangible law of nature requires that something of those left behind always remains to tell the tale, although the telling may take a thousand years."

Remembering those words, she broke with the past, and sighting beyond the fallen walls of the townsite, she looked upon a gentle elevation of earth surrounded by some sickly trees. Leaving her pack at the collapsed entranceway to the main building, she set forth.

Finding and following the twin depressions of the ancient road, she soon was able to make out the white marble obelisk proclaiming the way to the choice spot in Locust Grove where Molly Morehouse—she was a Texan—buried her beloved Jake over the protest of the New Believers, who objected to a Socialist drunk being buried on the elevated center ground reserved for their own, insisting that Jake be disposed of in an undeveloped corner set aside for such cases. But Molly, whose father had served in the Confederate Army under General Sibley, raised such a rukus that the purple-shirters gave in, and Jake was laid to rest at the highest point in the cemetery with the Reverend Zebulon Montgomery Gonzalez himself conducting the service. Furthermore, Molly blew the insurance money on the "biggest damn tombstone in New Mexico." She reckoned if an ineradicable spirit still haunted La Flor, it was the defiant ghost of the Texas woman who ran the Lone Star rooming house and cafe.

Pausing to blow a minute—she had been walking too fast—she looked upon the advancing old graveyard in reverential solemnity, for she had attended several burials there. Outstanding, of course, was the extraordinary internment of Jake Morehouse, whose majestic, tapering monument beckoned the way. Nearing, she recognized metamorphic rock stumps resting in the dubious shade of moribund locust trees, telling where fallen Woodmen slept. Scattered here and there were sagging or prone stone markers, unpainted wooden crosses and lonely mounds unmarked save by tumbleweeds, ant hills, and silence in the sun.

Wrapped in gray sadness, she stood in a moment of melancholy humility, remembering that the family plot back at home lay no less desolate. So preoccupied with emotionalism she became that she didn't see the fence until she walked right up to it. Entry to Locust Grove Cemetery was denied by a commanding, ten-foot, chain-link fence, incurving at the top and bearing an official shield with the warning:

DANGER!   EXPLOSIVES!   —   PELIGRO!   EXPOSIVOS!
TESTING AREA

Wounded in spirit, short-changed and sick to her stomach, she turned her back on the mute cemetery and the cold, inflexible restraint that had taken command. She wanted to run away, and did.

17

Back at the ashes of La Flor, Virgil was waiting with her burden strapped to his strong shoulders. Hand-in-hand they set out across the resilient epidermis of flaxen pasture grass. Miles and miles they traveled side by side, days, months, years. Then his footprints veered away, and she felt the total burden on her own shoulders, which at first recoiled and then straightened up, for she knew she must in human loneliness march awandering to her own drum. Being pregnant sure didn't make it any easier.

Shooing the past away, or trying to, anyway, she picked up the main trail that plowed a friendly furrow past La Mesita and out across the easy corduroy plain, reminding her, as good roads sometimes did that as a worthy pilgrim she should emerge from the dark cave where lay the detritus of broken dreams, into the sunshine of delectable quest. And feeling the salubrious caress of a mild breeze on her face, in her heart, she bade the visit into the past find its niche in the past. Time had called the tune and put the fiddle away.

La Flor was just another ghost town. She had visited many such forfeited settlements on her rounds—Madrid, La Bajada, Cabezon, Elizabethtown, Waldo. La Flor could be any of them, except that its fallen walls were curiously stained with purple.

One morning the terrain began to lose something of its monotony. The loamy, earth supported scrub cedars and junipers, and away out yonder to the north, stood a handsome stand of blueberry-colored mountains. Various bypaths hitched on to the trail giving it breadth, spirit and a sense of destination. In about five miles, maybe six, she halted before a sign post of ancient vintage and the worse for wear and tear. The wooden arm beckoning the way to Chilili was in poor shape. The unwritten law of the trail excused an occasional redotted "i" if the indicated designation remained legible. But three "i's" lined up with only a couple of "l's" between were sitting ducks for the pistol-toting wayfarer, especially if he had had a few. The pathetic Chilili sign was so bullet-punctured it was doubtful whether a stranger looking for the little community in the Manzanos would ever find it.

An independent sign tacked to an alternate arm of the post caught her eye. Inscribed wavelets accompanied by a drawn arrow foretold a source of water down a barely definable side road. An interesting thing was that the wavelets had been crossed out, indicating that where water had been, there was none now. A source of water being an environmental necessity for any trail, curiosity over the dry-up raised its hand, asking to be heard. She waved it aside, moving on with a twinge of reluctance, for deep in her bones there bestirred a haunting feeling that the withered old ruts of the byroad led to something of more than ordinary interest. When a glitter of steely light caught her eye, the climate of presage became established. The oblique glisten definitely betokened something more substantial than the reflection of the sun's rays on a tin can.

As if yielding to the pull of a loadstone, she turned back the few steps to the juncture, where she turned off on the down-sloping, weed-infested side road, feeling while she walked as if she were wrapping a thread on a spindle that ultimately would reveal a prize. After about a hundred yards the trace aligned itself with an old railroad track. Both long unused avenues of commerce loosely paralleled a waterless stream bed that wore the ash-white complexion of death. Her soul was touched by the pathetic plight of the once clear, clean watercourse that had been caught in the clutches of an insatiably thirsty, incredibly lovely, henna-pink jungle. Now she knew why the wavelets on the crossroads sign had been exed out. The precious melted snow from the high mountains no longer provided water for man, animals, and the growing things upon which they fed. All had been forfeited to the ravenous thirst of an ornamental shrub whose prolific progeny had played havoc with the ecology of the land, sucking moisture from live streams, leaving their beds arid, bitter, and overseasoned with salt.

The old road and the railroad tracks soon separated, the tracks by their rigid nature pursuing a beeline while she and the wagonway followed the snaky course of the ill-favored stream. Pushing her way through the feathery, pastel-tinted racemes of bordering tamarisks, she tried to assess the cause of man's feckless devaluation of the earth's bounty. Were such scenes of grevious damage the results of foolish, unripe judgment? Had man undertaken to achieve his purpose before the kinks in his structure had been ironed out? Were such despoilments of the earth's blessings as the planting of salt cedars, the slaughter of the buffalo, the destroying of grass texture, the axing of timbers, the unthinkable establishment of weapon testing ranges, results of headlong strides of an immature civilization not yet dry behind the ears? Or, on the other hand, had it come to pass that man's fitness to run things was so pooped and worn out that any old thing might happen any time, anywhere? Sure was something to think over.

The old road caught up with the railroad tracks at an abandoned settlement of some half a hundred old frame houses, all desolate and sagging in neglect. Their plight was discouraging. It seemed as if this miserable little brood of houselets had crawled to this unhallowed spot from some multiparous litter, unfolding identical drab front porches as they came, only to wither in their wooden shells in a season of drought, famine, and despair.

Two more durable monuments to a happier day, however, looked down in mute resignation upon this graveyard of broken dreams, an enormous old cottonwood—she had seen only one other of comparable branch and girth, the one standing and having stood on the spacious hard dirt plaza at San Ildefonso Pueblo longer than time remembered—and the ticket to oblivion, an abandoned railway depot. The venerable tree under whose armpit the rust-red tile roof of the deserted station found shelter would be the last to go. Cottonwoods were made that way. The gray stucco shell it defended from ill winds would last less long, but through it, something of the history of this ghostly community might be uncovered.

Having been properly brought up, she addressed herself to the old depot. "My name is Leaf McIntosh. How do you do?"

There was no response. How could there be? The station had no name. She looked upon the bare facade in utter disbelief. Never before had she encountered a ghost town so far along the steps going down that its name had been lost. Even Waldo, New Mexico, had a name.

The town's complete loss of identity touched her soul. Obviously, more than one hundred human beings had walked these weed-clogged streets when there were no weeds. Residents hung chili ristras beside their doorways, and danced La Cuna on a platform on the plaza on Saturday night. On Sunday morning when the bell tolled, they went to church. Now, all was empty and silent. If this inhabitation appeared on a map at all, it rated no more than a dot and a question mark. The more thought she devoted to the town's plight, the deeper became her personal obligation to rescue this dispeopled settlement from geographic oblivion. Surely somewhere among the debris lay a clue to its identity.

Leaving the Two Grey Hills on the station platform, she poked among the weeds and fallen timbers, finding no trace of anything that suggested the town's name. Piqued by disappointment, she turned back toward the depot only to stumble and come within an inch of falling into a thistle bed obscuring a prone, iron well pump, its useless arm resting at its side. Attached to the mute lever by a length of baling wire was a shiny tin cup, as spanking clean as the day it had left the hardware store.

A bright idea dawned. In its own way the cup showed a willingness to cooperate by holding still while she untwisted the wires attaching it to the pump's handle. Tenderly cuddling the shining chalice to her breast, she began searching the rubble for a sound piece of board on which she could letter a sign. All oddments of plank she turned over were, unfortunately, furred and rotten.

Returning to the portico of the depot, she sat on a wrought iron bench eternally beolted to the cement floor to think things over. The cup that she held as tenderly as The Grail seemed to be thinking right along with her. It seemed to her that a latent spark of spirit had slept in the town pump's cup during all those years of desolation waiting to be relumed by some sweet circumstance. Thus the obligation to restore the ghostly premises to an identifiable entity offered even greater challenge. With renewed enthusiasm, she set forth to search the area for a suitable sign board.

She didn't have to go far. Loosely hanging from the waiting room wall was just what she needed, a wooden sign setting forth regulations on spitting in both English and Spanish. She hoped the railroad company wouldn't mind unorthodox use of the aviso. After all, it was obvious that the depot had for many years been solely patronized by squirrels, lizards, insects, rats, and snakes. While some of these critters had a habit of spitting, the addiction was not subject to official restraint because they could not read. Presumably, they couldn't—not New Mexican ones anyway.

Already having her eye on a potential instrument of pry and percussion—a loosened iron spike standing head and shoulders above a disintegrating wooden crosstie—she got down to business. With the unyielding determination of a horse dentist, she banged the iron tooth back and forth with a rock until it let go. Prying the spitting sign off the waiting room wall was as easy as pie. In the process she was careful to protect the alignment of five good nails that creaked complaint on being yanked out backwards—and who could blame them? Having a special purpose for those nails, she put them aside.

The back side of the old sign was clean, smooth and inviting. Nothing presents greater challenge to human nature than a piece of clean board when you have a pencil in your pocket. She could hardly wait to begin. She knew how to letter. Heaven only knew why. It was just one of those little gratuities nature occasionally tosses into the embryo sac rather than down the drain.

Digging through her skirt pockets and producing her old stub of cedar pencil, she accurately spaced and outlined her message. With a selected nugget of charcoal taken from those abundantly inhabiting the vicinity of the railroad tracks, she was able to heighten legibility. Next, using the spike head as a hammer, she drove the fifth nail aslant above the centerline of the wording, fashioning it into a sturdy hook. Creation of the sign was a labor of love, and if she did say so herself, an excellent job was turned out. So far, so good! The real test of her ingenuity would come in securing the sign in a properly balanced position on the facade of the depot, vis-a-vis the cross buck where the passing world would see.

Rising a-tiptoe, she held the sign up as far as she could, temporarily cinching it with a single nail to get the effect. Moving back, she looked upon her masterpiece with a cold, evaluating eye. It was not in harmonious perspective, but it would have to do because she had started to cough, so she banged the nails in.

Overexertion reactivated pesky glottal explosions that had bothered her off and on ever since she had pneumonia the winter she lived in a cave on Pajarito Canyon. A few moments of relaxation while she drank sunshine did the trick. And she knew that while the trusty old sun delivered the goods all around the world, it saved its brightest and best for New Mexico.

Feeling better, she moved back to observe the established designation from the stance of a spectator. Magnifico! The nameless, the forgotten, the disinherited had been rescued from the abyss of oblivion. In the nick of time, some precious metaphysics had ineluctably drawn her feet to this hapless, hopeless settlement that was going down for the third time. Naturally she was proud of her contribution—doubly proud. Not only had she performed a noble achievement for historical record, she had borned a work of art. Beaming with self-esteem she observed the cup hanging from the hook, and below it the words:

TIN CUP

NEW MEXICO

Population 1

Looking pridefully upon the capital achievement, she reckoned that Grandma, under kindred circumstance, would have thumbed to her personal leaf near the end of her Bible—right after Births—Deaths—and would have registered a fresh, pencil-drawn star for her crown, another of many.

The dear old soul had devoted a lifetime of deed and song directed toward eventual occupation of a golden throne with a gem-studded diadem on her head. At Granny's funeral the congregation had sung, "Will There Be Any Stars In My Crown?" And she, at the age of nine, had wondered why there should be any question.

Her gesture of goodwill toward Tin Cup naturally was rendered without expectation of a sometime award. The joy of fulfillment was enough. Maybe it had been for Grandma, too.

It was time to hit the trail again. Shadows were lengthening, and the feverish sun was about to draw a curtain around its bed. She must hurry. But when she was about to set forth, something deep in the roots of her human self whispered that the tie to Tin Cup was too close, too personal, to be hastily terminated. The premonitive feeling presented its case in brass tacks terms. Here in Tin Cup she was on familiar ground, obviating the chore of hunting a place to camp. The platform of the depot would make a firm bed, no lumps, no rocks, no cockleburs. In case of inclement weather there would be a roof. As for food, across the tracks a stand of ripe prickly pears beckoned. That did it!

She slept like a log that night, awakening to behold a dawn of rose geranium and Guadalupe blue. The new day revealed an inspired village. Rescued from oblivion, inspired by provable documentation of geographic existence, Tin Cup, New Mexico held its head high.

18

After breakfasting well on what she thought must be the most delicious cactus apples in the southwest, she rested for a spell. It was not without reluctance that she would resume the journey, for in those few hours of residence, she had come to look on Tin Cup as home. "I won't look back," she said to herself, "I'll just bravely walk away."

Abruptly, she quickly covered her eyes with cupped palms as a spate of sharp sand and nettle chaff engulfed the depot. The retreat of the capricious whirlwind was as sudden as its assault. Looking up, blinking billious spots from her eyes, she watched the spinning funnel cycle down the glistening railroad track into nothing.

Getting to her feet to whoosh dust and chaff from her skirt, a weather-worn piece of paper fell from her lap. Snatching it away from the devilish backlash of the twister, she saw it contained printing. In spite of the faded, brittle condition of the paper, its message was easily legible:

NOTICE!

All pilgrims making the journey in quest of final Truths are directed to assemble at Leaning Rock no later than September 30. Mass pilgrimage to Revelatory Mountain will begin at dawn October 1.

Signed:

Rev. Erasumus Judd

Over and over, she read the message, testing its bona fides, making sure that what she held in her hand, the hand itself, and the mind that read the message were not under the subtle influence of a waking dream. Finally convinced of the inerrancy of this document, she sat still, humble and heavy with gratitude.

During the years of her pilgrimage, and they were many, she had often times been favored by manifestations, lured on by their beckonings, but what her heart had hungered for most always had receded into "sometime." Now this small piece of ragged paper delivered by one of nature's swiftest couriers, this precious consolation that she pressed against her heart, presented the first tangible evidence that culmination of her quest was near at hand. She must set forth.

Then a distressing shadow darkened her path. Suppose the end of September had come and gone? "If Lillian were only here," she lamented, but with a less impassioned thought, realized that the date pad under Lillian's appealing picture had been torn off, used up ere they met, leaving only the timeless representation of her unexampled beauty of face and form to linger through the years in after-token. Especially over bars.

Her innate attunement to nature's rhythmic rounds had long ago obviated the uninspiring chore of flipping a calendar page or winding a clock. When the sun went down, and so far it always had, she made her bed. If she woke up in the night she got a pretty good idea what time it was from the position of the moon. The lark or some other bird or nosey vermint generally told her when to get up, and if not, the sun again accommodated. During the day, of course, she was her own "shadder stick." The seasons identified themselves, albeit loosely, through weather conditions, colors, fruits, dress of fellow creatures, bird flights, hibernations, and matings— all interesting when you come to know them.

None of these observable phenomena, however, could pin point a specific date such as she needed to know. Being somewhat of a realistic turn of mind, she realized that she had to draw on her own reservoir of resourcefulness, and mighty quick.

She began considering some of nature's inherent indications of time passage. The first one that came to mind was the wild gourd method. If the lighter of its longitudinal stripes had a look of parchment, autumn was well on the way. If putty-colored, whether the leaves had curled or not, frost had its foot in the door. A proper specimen lay ready for the taking along the uncleared shoulder of the railroad track.

It was a pretty thing, looking not unlike a miniature watermelon. The initial green of its dominate stripes had faded to the shade of ripe peas, and the yellowish alternates had a look of old ivory. Careful not to injure its tendril tie, she turned the little gourd clockwise in her hand and observed the underbelly to be the color of tallow, the color of harvest—September. So far, so good. But not good enough.

Next she decided to use the thump test, knowing the more mature the pith and seeds, the duller would be the percussive response. The resounding thump echoed like the plop of an over-ripe apple as it hit the ground. She figured the gourd's maturing process had reached the vicinity of the last week in September. Still, she needed confirming proof.

It came in a most extraordinary manner. A squirrel was cautiously emerging from the weeds, sniffing in closer and closer. She stood utterly still, letting him come as near as he chose. When about five, maybe five and a half feet away, he stood at attention, directing his unblinking little buckshot eyes to survey the totality of the scene, as if he intended to go back and make a report.

Whatever intelligence he may have gained could scarcely match what he disclosed, for she was observing him, too. The downy gray hairs showing in the tufts of his ears foretold imminent frost. At this altitude a freeze could be expected as early as the last week in September. Too close for comfort. She moved, and so did the squirrel.

A waning September was further indicated by the southward track of the sun and the yellowing leaves of the old cottonwood. She was almost one hundred percent certain that the date lay between the twenty-third and the thirtieth. Counting the days off on her fingers to get their feel, she sensed a tremor of memory's needle. After fluctuating a bit, it hung on the twenty-fourth, a date that bestirred from long slumber. This was her birthday! This was her simpatico day, her day of good omen!

With only six days to reach Leaning Rock and join fellow pilgrims on the final phase of her magnificent quest, there wasn't a minute to lose. In three shakes—inappropriately of a dead lamb's tail—she was packed and ready to go. But at the last moment she was delayed by a reminder of unfinished business.

Discarding her trappings and finding her pencil, she went over to the sign and reworked the population figure from one into a lop-sided zero. Then she shouldered her pack and headed for intersection with the main trail, where she found room at the bottom of the Chilili sign to add a postscript:

TIN CUP — Left 1 mi.

The sky was cloudless, the air fresh. As she swung down the trail she thought what good walking weather it was—really the best she had met with in quite a spell. She spurred her feet to make the most of it. Just the same, she paused occasionally to scan the western horizon for the tilted landmark. It was nowhere in sight.

After traveling several hours, a curious turn of the trail directed her way through a clutch of up-thrust, butter-colored rocks some of them quite lofty, and placed so close together, the trail had to draw in to slip through. While negotiating with one of these narrow passes, she happened to look up. She got the surprise of her life.

Sitting calmly in the high, bright sun atop the righthand slice of limestone wall was a mature mountain lioness. Motionless, her tawny lean body rested in the saffron glow of declining day, her tail curled around front paws like a contented house cat. The great cat looked down. Their eyes met in a moment of empathy and peace. Then the feline's lithe body leaped overhead across the cleft and was gone—just a fleeting moment of emotional identification between two of nature's vanishing species who met and passed at a remote crossroads on a minute particle of cosmic dust.

Before long, the trail began to skirt the downward edge of the talus of a limestone wall. Being on the weary side, and with the day about to ring down the curtain, she responded to a vacancy offered by a wind-scoured hollow high up on the cliffside. It was no problem to locate the footholds laid out by the Pueblos, who were indefatigable climbers. Propelling her laden frame from step to step without an Indian's savvy was something else again. Pausing for a breather halfway up the Indian ladder, she looked back on the cloud-canopied trail, feeling a twinge of conscience for seeking an alien roof when there was no climatic urgency. Or was there? By the time she had cleared the final foothold, the northeast wind was pushing dark clouds down the mountain slopes, and she could smell the change.

The inner space of the cave was limited so she had to hinge her knees to fit into the spread Two Grey Hills, but she was grateful for the shelter. If by chance it did rain—it sometimes does in New Mexico—why, let it. It would take some gully washer to flood this high. Being utterly pooped from the upward climb, she was only peripherally aware of a distant roll of the tater wagon. She closed her eyes, and an overhead spider began to weave.

A new day already was at hand when she suddenly started to get up and answer Tiger's scratching at the door, only to discover that she actually had been awakened by the clear-cut staccato of sleet pellets against a surface of rock wall. Acquainted with the formal pattern of southwestern sleet showers, she listened. As she knew it would, right in the middle of a violent bombardment somebody threw the switch, shutting the whole thing off. Just like that!

Reaching out of the cave's entrance as she had done from the dugout door when a child, she scooped up a handful of icy white globules, hungrily consuming them from a cold, wet palm. There was nothing more refreshing than clean, new sleet—unless, of course, it was fresh sleet seasoned with a bit of milk, sugar, and perhaps a dash of cinnamon.

By the time she had finished breakfast and geared for descent, all visible traces of the icy ground cover had melted away, but the afterbreath lingered, assuring invigorating weather for travel. After her muscles and bones recovered from a night of awkward position, she made the most of it.

On this 25th day of September, with only five more days to go, the trail put the rugged terrain behind and took out across a flat, grassy vega dancing under the sun. On the rim of the plain she could see shining lakes and other objects. Figuring nature was up to its hocuspocus again, she kept her eyes on the road. Later on, she happened to look up again and could clearly make out a group of persons, some twenty five or more, proceeding single file along the shore of a long lake, their shadows sharply imaged in the bright water as they pursued an oblique course that eventually would converge with her own.

Cheered by the warm feeling of becoming a member of a commonly destined body of truth seekers journeying to Leaning Rock, her steps quickened, accelerating in direct ratio to her galloping anticipation. Then, of course, she began to pant and cough. Desperately in need of water, she started to get the canteen, but found it wasn't necessary.

Now if anybody in the world, except maybe a Bible student, had told her this, she would have pointed to her cranium and twirled a finger. But right there on the shoulder of the trail stood a healthy shrub, hung with mouth-watering, saffron-yellow fruits veined with red. The ripest of the wild plums had fallen already and lay on the hard ground. She lost no time in taking and slaking, expectorating the seeds for birds and other animals, of course.

With thirst, hunger, and the cough assuaged at the same time, she filled her pockets with the firmer plums for supper and reoccupied her burden. But when she set out again, there was no trace of the other pilgrims, not even the swirl of their dust. Figuring they must be transiting depressed terrain, she began scouting the plain for an elevation where she could get an overall view of the total surroundings. With luck, she would then locate the crusaders with whom she felt a deep kinship of purpose.

The only thing of any height within range of vision was a good size sand dune dozing in intense sunlight about a mile, maybe a mile and a half, ahead. It became her target.

But dadgummit, that dune was more than twice as far ahead as she had been led to believe, and it wasn't very big either. Furthermore, it was a good half mile off trail, and the untraced way looked mighty chancey. But she was so anxious to locate the fellow travelers she took a swig from the canteen and headed duneward.

She hadn't gone more than fifty yards off-trail when she was stopped cold by a metallic shudder of interlocking joints. In a nearby dusty arena, a battle to death was in progress. With fists clenched in tension, she watched a bird that always acted as if it didn't have a grain of gumption, blind the hypnotic eye of a rattler with rushes of sand and finish him off. The cold, congenital aptitude for surgery inherent in the clownish roadrunner was something she had never been able to comprehend. No less incredible, however, was the native ability of the same snake to hypnotize and swallow certain susceptible creatures, even those who could fly.

She pondered the strange bird-reptile fixation into which nature had invested considerable voodoo, but she had to admit that she had never been able to unriddle it. Only an Indian could. In cautious apprehension, she proceeded toward the apex of the subtly fortified dune. Then the air became vitiated by the acetic aroma exuded by a whip-tail vinegaroon who had been disturbed by her footfall and she breathed easier, knowing the way to be sanitized and clear.

Short of breath and oozing sweat, she finally gained the crest of the dune. After spelling a while, she ripped off a wild gourd leaf, and using it as a sunshade, she surveyed the total circumference of the earth's rim. There was no trace of the other pilgrims. None whatsoever.

Discouraged, and with a twinge of remorse for not having made herself known to them while they were in sight, she began scouting for a less complicated way back to the waiting trail. From the looks of things, she would have better footing and save time by taking the alternate leg of the triangle.

True, the chosen way was less plagued by weeds and the critters they harbored, but when she stepped out on an eliptical barren area that she had taken for an old buffalo wallow, the soil felt strange underfoot. Very strange. Pretty soon, it seemed curiously moist and of the consistency of talcum—dirty, gummy talcum redolent of ashes. But she kept on going.

A little better than half way across, she became awkwardly aware that her tracks were filling in as soon as she left them. This caused some uneasiness, but she continued on, treading as lightly as she could with a load on her back, knowing the while an inbalance, even a cough, might trigger disaster. Just as the ashy sand began pouring over her right boot top, she sighted the shore. But it was some fifty yards farther off.

19

She put on her thinking cap, the one with the orange plume, and her native aptitude for survival promptly got on the ball, turning up with an idea that, although on the far-fetched side, just might work. Even if she couldn't swim, she knew how to float.

While her feet tugged ahead on their own, she directed her fingers to untie the romals girding the Two Grey Hills and remove the drill pouch containing provisions and personal items. When the awkward canteen was somehow cinched to the bag, she hitched the unit to her belt, completely freeing the Navajo blanket for a purpose.

Then came the crucial stroke, and not a moment too soon. Her free hands swung the Two Grey Hills into the air, letting it settle outspread at her feet. Leaning forward, she lowered her accoutered body to the blanket. Stretching out full length, she then bade her bony fingers draw the edges of the slowly sinking blanket about her body. When enshrouded, she executed a sideways lurch for momentum and began to roll and float, roll and float, in the easy rhythmic advance of a barrel on a lake.

Eventually the strange cocoon began to lose drag, and the nervous tremble of the gummy undertow phased out in direct ratio to the retexturing of stable soil. And Glory Hallelujah, she rolled ashore!

The entegumental envelope burst and never was fresh, clean air more gratefully taken, nor was the Source of Things more devoutly thanked. Safe in port, she quickly pushed the canvas accouterments sack aside and let go a coughing spell she had sought so hard to contain. Reaching for a gourd leaf, she wiped the uppage, and sat for a moment of respite while she studied the unholy map of her barely-achieved course. She thought she could detect a beguiling smile on its countenance. She was certain of it when right before her eyes the shuddering gray sands actively smoothed the wrinkles out, leaving a surface as inviting as a crockful of clabber. Ready to deny everything, she supposed. Well, that was that.

Somehow she felt sort of puny-like, but realizing her schedule was behindhand, she decided to get up and pick up the trail anyway. But when she tried to stand, she couldn't. She plopped back down. Her head swam and she felt nauseous. She tried to get up again, and again, but her legs gave way like homemade stilts. Sitting there on the innocent, runty grass bordering Satan's fishing hole, she wondered what in the world was the matter with her. She had never been affected this way before.

Presently a dear old friend whispered something in her ear, something she wouldn't know about. So she relaxed and waited. Pretty soon the needle of normalcy fluttered and grooved and she recovered her landlegs. Captain Ahab was right! It was seasickness.

Despite all that dither and ado, she was surprised to find that suddenly she was hungry. Feeling in the pockets of her skirt, she produced four ruptured but edible wild plums that somehow had managed to survive the unorthodox transit of the quicksand slough. Upon consuming the juicy fruits and properly spitting the seeds, she felt quite satisfied, and began preparations to proceed. Removing and emptying her boots, she let them air while she quirt-flipped ashy powder from the firm weave of the Two Grey Hills. Shod and packed, she took a farewell look at the clabber crock.

She had heard tales about such eddying, sand-filtering traps, but this was her first, and please God may it be her last, encounter with one. Someday that slowly creeping dune lying to the east, the one she had vainly employed as a lookout, would obliterate the shifting sand mass. Luckily, her bones would not lie at the bottom of the hourglass, entombed in underworld slush with those who didn't make it across.

"My God! Could Uncle John be down there?" He got on his horse and rode off one day, saying he was going to look at some land, and that was the last anybody ever heard of him. "Poor Uncle John! Bye, Uncle John! Maybe you didn't deliberately abandon Aunt Birdie and the kids after all."

By the time she caught up with the mainstream of the Cross Plains Trail, it was midafternoon and quite hot, although with the approach of the fifth point of Libra when summer burns its bridges, not unseasonably so. She paused occasionally to wipe briny sweat from her brow and reconnoiter, but there was no trace of the other pilgrims. None whatsoever.

She tried to jolly her mind into believing the group had wisely taken shelter from the biting sun in some manzanita thicket, and in due time would emerge into view. But inwardly she was unsure. She was only cursorily aware of in-feeding paths and foot trails, their habit being to latch on to the main road for a few miles and then branch off for their own purpose. Pretty soon it came to her attention that the trail was being coattailed by all manner of byroads and animal walks, preindicant of squeezed passage, say a bridge or a vado. So she was not surprised when some distance ahead she sighted a raw arroyo that ran across the even plain like a crack in a plate.

Presently she could tell that the trail was heading for some sort of dual scaffolding standing out in high perspective on the tight, shimmering skyline. Upon approach, these crude brackets turned out to be stone abutments standing face to face across a deep gully, with nothing between them except New Mexico's air and sunshine. In some lost time the span had gone hell-bent for the Rio Grande, leaving the disjoined buttresses to hang on the best way they could until help came. Not that it mattered much as far as commerce was concerned. Thwarted wheel and hoof had contrived a circumventing dry ford that over the years had accommodated so much moving traffic that the arroyo banks had eroded into a readily navigable crossing.

The only trouble was that this by-pass had ruptured certain natural retaining walls, permitting flash flood run-off to spill over, creating a system of silt sluices emptying into depressions. Still feeling the sting of the set-to with the quicksand sink, she was leary of these waterless estanques, sun-cracked and curling like old shingles.

Lucky for her the trail not only managed to stay out of trouble, but it pulled away to the south, penetrating a level area of gramma, spiny cacti, and cholla. The terrain was so flat a person could see for eight or ten miles. At one point, she saw or thought she could see, some people moving on the far hoop of earth and sky. Her steps quickened in anticipation of contact with the elusive fellow pilgrims, but the only indications of prior transit she came across were tags of white filament on mesquite bushes. There was no sight or sound of life except her own.

Day declined. The retreating sun cast an amber glow on the quiet earth, dappled here and there with dark shadows lengthening from slim yucca stalks. Her personal silhouette was a tall, plodding crone with a bundle of faggots on her back. When the rim of the plain was scanned for a wisp of smoke from a campsite, the old hag paused, too, porching her witch's brow in sardonic mimicry. It got to be annoying, and she wished the ridiculous shadow would go away and let her alone, for this had been a hard day. But toe-to-toe the witch hung on like a bad conscience, right up to the time when all shadows were one.

The sky became a great garden of cabbages and wary of what might be in the cards, she immediately made camp. Even before she finished her supper of nuts, bulbs, and seeds, an ominous, chilly silence lay on the land. Knowing now what was coming up, she hugged her arms, wondering what in the world could have happened to her sweater.

In about twenty minutes, maybe half an hour, the sky darkened, and a teeth-chattering wind shuddered the gramma's fragile sickles. Rolling up in the Indian blanket, she called it a day.

How often her family had done just that when a blue norther stalked the plains. Her mind picked up the clue.

Grandpa hollered, "She's acomin'," and hurried to shut the windmill off. The other men began working like beavers, tying down and locking up everything that could take off with the wind. Mama brought the washing in, dry or not, and I grabbed the washtub that would like nothing better than to join the vanguard of fleeting tumbleweeds. I rolled the galvanized tub inside the henhouse and bolted the door that was used only by people. The chickens had their own come-and-go opening at which they already were flocked, although they could not possibly have seen what was boiling up over the rim of the prairie. Maybe they could smell the storm, or maybe they figured from a darkening sky that roosting time was coming up. Chickens can think. They're not dumb like turkeys. Although they're not as smart as pigs.

With everything braced for the blow, we huddled on the hard bare earth in front of Grandpa's dugout, where he was king and his half-buried castle was our refuge. Our eyes were focused on the awesome dark cloud that was moving in. We waited as one for that moment of mingled ecstasy and bravado that would come seconds before we would rush down the steps, slam the door, shut the windows, and let her blow!

We used to wrap up in comforters, horse blankets, quilts—anything we could find—and bed down on the hard dugout floor waiting for the hellacious norther to blow itself out. We rarely spoke. We just lay there listening to the guy wires scrape against the stove pipe like a sick, country fiddle. Sometimes at night it would get so cold we could hear the shells of the cackle berries in the crate back of the stove go pop-pop-pop as they froze and cracked.

As a rule the wind allayed around dawn. Grandpa always was the first one up—he never slept well except on his bunk in the barn—and he'd insert the lifter into each stove eye, tilting it gently to let the accumulation of snuff-colored dust slide off into the fire well. Then he would build a roaring corncob fire. Crawling out next, Mama would put the coffee pot on and whip up cornbread batter, and early spring life on the Staked Plains would go on as usual.

Now, in September, she suspected the gale would be less frigid and blow less long. In a couple of hours, it all was over. Hungry for the companionship of her beloved stars, she bared her face to the gray-black sky, bidding the few stars under purview to gather up their friends and come low for an interlude of friendly communication. This they did, sparkling as they cautiously lowered in disciplined unison. Even so, one occasionally tripped and fell.

Having been a trusted friend of the stars for so many years, she confidentially asked whether they were beginning to feel the irresistible pull of the Fifth Mesa, now preciously near. They sparkled that they did. She had a lot more to talk over with them, but she couldn't keep awake.

As often the case on a cold night, she overslept. She was not awakened by the usual knock of the day star at Heaven's door, but by the wubbling complaint of an unfed coyote slinking back to his lair. Having faced breakfastless days herself, she thought about whistling the hungry fellow to come and share her nuts and bulbs. On a soberer note, though, she knew he already had sniffed her and retreated.

The new day's trail was in pretty fair shape, and for quite a spell she made good time. Then, as she somehow knew it would, the terrain began to lower and assume an agricultural posture, albeit with meager mood or spirit. Here and there the old road weaved past patches of withered cornstalks between whose once proud rows melons, beans, and squashes had grown. Each plot was accompanied by fallen adobe walls shaded by timeless grieving, golden-boughed cottonwoods that made the scene less desolate, as cottonwoods were born to do.

In the presence of an ageless, yellowing trailside tree, she came to a dead stop. "Saints and watermelons!" she cried.

Bedashed if she could remember how long ago it was when she had last visited this spot. And if it was as long ago as it had to be, she sure must have been traveling in circles for a heck of a long time.

She remembered the place well. Right over there was where she had stopped the buggy and dropped the hitch weight, and she and her little daughter, Ginny— long since married and living in Alaska—had gone over, hoping to buy squashes. Over here to the right had stood a makeshift wooden table displaying a dozen or so hand-carved, calmly-tolerating saints, some in robes and sandals and carrying staffs, others on horseback holding banners. A short distance away, on the left side of the tree, had been a spread, rainbow-hued Chimayo blanket displaying ripe watermelons. Between the exhibits a bilingual wooden sign had been nailed to the tree trunk announcing wares nutritive to both spirit and body:

SANTOS Y SANDIAS — SAINTS AND WATERMELONS

Sitting knees hinged on the bare earth with his back to the wall of tree had been woodcarver-gardener, Patricio Ortega, sound asleep with his sombrero shading his face.

Not wishing to interrupt the siesta of the venerable vendor who had no squashes anyway, she and Ginny had driven away. But she never forgot the incident, or Patricio Ortega, who was the richest man she ever knew. Although his pockets had been empty, he was blessed by something all the money in the world couldn't buy—solitude of the soul.

Around midday on the 26th of September, infeeding paths and byroads began to emerge through rabbitbrush and yucca, giving the ancient trail width and self-command. Sure of itself, it was letting the world of commerce know that its objective concerned some visibly chalk-stroked mountains ahead and to the right. Intersectional signs in their own arrow-twisting way advised the wayfarer that if he didn't qualify for the mountain pass, he should turn left and take the long way around to Leaning Rock. Because time was running low, she opted for the shortcut.

After pushing her ticklish way through a jungle of mountain willows, fuzzy-spiked cattails, and marsh grasses, she found herself on the gravelly bank of a quarter mile wide stream bed inhabited by sand, rocks, occasional silent pools, and a narrow flow of briskly moving water. No bridge? Oh, yes, there was, but like so many bridges in flash flood prone rural New Mexico, this one consisted only of a beginning and an end.

Figuring her chances of making it across were on the questionable side, she toyed with the idea of backtracking and taking the long road around, but realizing that in one way or another it, too, had to cross the same river, she reassessed the situation at hand. On the opposite side of the expansive bed she observed that the continuum of the moving thread of water swept closer to a gently elevated bank where the trail's traffic obviously emerged. She set target.

Taking her boots off and slipping them beneath the snug romals girding the Two Grey Hills, she lifted her skirts and began to jump, wade and in general negotiate a precarious way toward the main flow. At its copiously weeping bank, she ungallused and hurled her pack across. By Golly, it hit target! Then, backing up and running like the devil, she executed a wild leap. She almost made it. She could use a bath, all right, but what a way to take one!

Thrashing about in the icy water, she cried, "Help! Help! Somebody throw me a rope!" But the vast turquoise sky she addressed was as unhearing as oblivion.

Lucky for her, though, after a few floundering yards, she caught hold of an old log and managed to work her way out. She went upstream to the pack. It had come untied when it hit, and things were blowing every which way. Then she got chill—a real teeth-chatterer. But after lying wrapped up, wet clothes and all, in the Two Grey Hills, she soon stopped shivering.

Crawling out before she stank up the expensive blanket, checking the bushes to make certain no one was peeking, she stripped to her skin and spread everything to dry in the lowering sun. Then, hugging her food sack, an Adamless Eve turned in. Never having gone to bed naked on a river bank before—not in a mighty long time, anyway—she felt so body-conscious she couldn't get to sleep. It was just one of those nights, and she was glad when it was over.

20

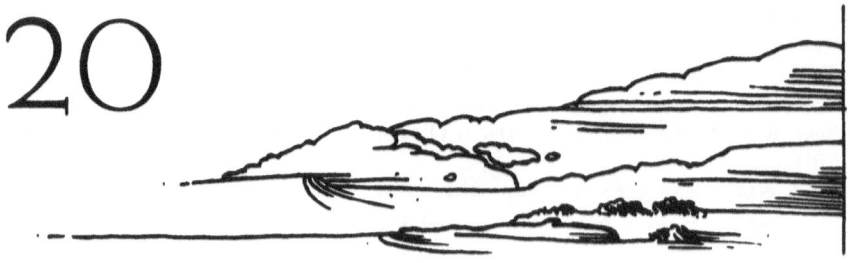

Surprisingly, in the morning when she dressed and assembled her scattered trappings, she never felt better, making her wonder whether a sleepless night occasionally might not be good for a person.

The new day she set forth upon was a honey. A soft matutinal breeze, more a whisper than a sigh, erased lingering traces of weariness from her eyes, letting her look upon the mountains, much nearer now. They were so blue they didn't seem to be at home on the earth, but on vacation from the sky. The sun was a pancake served with maple syrup—and who would not overlook a bit of slavering?

The trail on the 27th day of September left the river to meander through an area abundant in edible substances. Not knowing the prevailing disposition of high country ethniflora, she thought it a good idea to build up a reserve to carry her over the hump.

As she walked along she plucked jojoba acorns from overbending bushes, hand-cracking the tough shells between a couple of fist rocks, chewing the nutty mast for immediate or delayed swallowing. Ripe prickly pears beckoned from the roadside and she yanked them off with a yucca selvage, despining them on her boot soles and pocketing them for later consumption, only to toss several of the riper ones into her mouth from time to time, like a person with little will power does.

She acquired a traveling companion. Embarrassed by being caught off guard, she turned her face away to wipe cactus drool from her lips and chin. Meanwhile, the fellow wayfarer kept pace with her stride, turning from time to time to give her the one-eye out of the side of his puckish face. He provided cavalier escort for roughly half a mile, darting in and out of clumps of mesquite and rabbitbrush that he examined for mice and snakes, always managing somehow to keep no more than about twenty feet away. Occasionally, outstripping her pace, he would up his stiff tail as a brake until she caught up, peering at her with the tail of a lizard dangling from his silly mouth, in the impish challenge of a naughty child spoiling for a thrashing.

The roadrunner was a strange bird. In his presence she always had the peculiar feeling that his didoes disguised something hidden, allegorical, reminiscent of the mythopoeic concept of conflict between earth and sky. Maybe he was an offspring of the remote plumed serpent of the Aztec pantheon, who sailed westward promising to return. It was just a thought, but the analogy was there all right. Just look at him!

She wondered whether the strange earth-sky bird felt the near-presence of a third creature trotting on silent feet through the bushes, someone, even a chaparral cock couldn't outrun. But the spindle-legged clown had the situation under control. At the crucial moment, he upped his sky-wings, and soaring like a shied arrow, found haven in a distant clump of buckthron. The thwarted coyote then blended his lean gray body into the sage, the way coyotes do, and was gone.

When she reached the foothills of the shadowy lump of impeding mountain, the day was beginning to close. If a person wanted to keep on walking he could, for a round, nacreous moon held a torch. But she declined. A mountain was a critter she didn't hanker to tangle with at night. You never could tell what was going on in the mountain's mind, or what within its shadows stalked your scent. It was safer to look one straight in the eye in broad daylight.

Not that she had anything against mountains as such. They were put on earth like anything else, with a job to do, and they were turning out a steadfast, clean performance. Few of them even smoked. They were exalting to the spirit, especially from a distance, and one could not help but respect their monumentality and stubborn command. Besides, where else could Moses have found the Ten Commandments, or could Noah have anchored the Ark?

No, she didn't have any anti-mountain prejudice. She just reckoned that having been born and raised on the open aboveboard plains where you could see forever, she had always felt hemmed in and maybe a little bit suspicious on the few times life had taken her into the high country.

Memory leeched on, and she recalled how Dr. Baugh and she used to talk about man's umbilical tie to the land of his first mental functions. This was after the stroke, after he had surrendered office. She used to assist the enfeebled scholar to his leather recliner, elevate the foot rest, and gently lift each fragile leg to rest on it. Then she would sit on a stool at his side, or maybe on the floor at his feet, and they would drink tea and talk. He would speak of the day when, well or otherwise, he would leave the monotonous nowhereness of the plains and return to the low singing hills, the pines, the resounding coasts, the lucid streams of Maine, the resting place of his ancestors. In the end he had returned to the soil of the land of his birth. But it was "otherwise."

She also knew that in the mountains her heart, too, was a sojourner. Something elusive called "birthright" had eternally pledged it to Los Llanos Estacados, her immeasureable, beloved Staked Plains. When the trail entered the foothills, the sun was getting ready to close shop, and she wasn't a bit sorry. Having slept poorly the night before, she was ready to turn in as soon as she could find a clump of yucca for a campsite. Finding none, she explored for an alternate and came upon a foxtail pine that just might serve. A generous needle pad lay beneath a capacious branch-spread that would provide shelter from the silent snow showers that came early to the uplands.

But upon looking the situation over, she decided the accommodations offered by the pine were too gloom-ridden and chancy. She had tried a spot like that once in the Manzanos and what a night that was! Her rest had been tampered with, by dreams of rats—big rats, little rats, fat rats, lean rats, rats that walked on hind legs, rats that walked on forelegs with hind legs in the air, rats that waltzed in pairs with paper hats on. No, never again would she bed down under the branches of a foxtail pine.

101

And not entirely because of the ratty dream experience. Turkey buzzards roosting on the limbs were real. And they didn't care what they did or where they did it.

Scouting in the pure moonlight, she located an open area surrounded by a ring of gray-green junipers, yet explosed to the Heavens. "Tec-nos-pos" the Indians called it, where trees grow in a circle. She knew at once that this was the spot, and with a feeling of confidence, she spread her couch at the center point of the enclosure.

Snuggly bedded down in the caressing folds of the Navajo blanket with only her face exposed, she invited her friends, the stars, to emerge for conversation. But they were shy about coming down, apparently intimidated by the superior candle power of a moon in full, naked disc. But pretty soon an observing wisp of cloud took a hand in the matter, blowing smoke on the moon's face. Then, twinkling as they came, the stars moved down close to listen. She gave them the exciting tiding that according to calculation, in three more days she should arrive at Leaning Rock and become a member of an organized pilgrimage whose next stop would be the Fifth Mesa, where humanity's true destiny would be revealed.

She had a lot more to discuss but fatigue began fooling around with her thoughts, and pretty soon she didn't think at all. She was involved in a most strange dream. She was back home, humming and chording "Jesus Lover of my Soul" on the old pump organ in the front room, the largest of three rooms built onto the dugout the year the hail beat the wheat into sluice ice, but it was insured. An acquaintance, Herman Smith was his name, heard her playing and knocked on the door, wanting a drink of water.

Pleased to see Herman, she walked to the windmill with him and held the filled gourd dipper to his lips while he drank. He went his way, and she returned to the pump organ, this time chording and humming "Red Wing."

The dream was interrupted by a rustling of nearby branches. Awake and in possession of consciousness, she knew she had never known a man named Herman Smith in her whole life. Randall Smith, yes, but no Herman. Moreover, the face in the dream would scarcely be found on a human being anyhow. Yet, between them there had been neighborly harmony. Now according to Grandma's Dream Book, there always was a why and wherefore for a dream, bizarre and fanciful though it be. She was trying to put the pieces together when there came a further rustle of branches, this time accompanied by the hoof-stir of large animal as his legs expanded for natural reasons. Everything fell into place when the night air was pervaded by a strong caustic aroma nostalgic of the old homestead corral. She had a good laugh. When she had been around fourteen or so, Daddy owned a good-natured saddle horse named Herman Smith after a previous owner.

Reaching for the menthol jar, she screwed the lid down tight to conserve its waning strength. No baneful influence would intrude where wild mustangs billeted. As she settled down for some more sleep, she hoped the horses would be still there when she woke up. Being a former ranchwoman herself, she would like to make their acquaintance.

But when daylight came, their camp was empty. Looking back down the trail she saw them on their way to the river, an unclaimed and unclaimable draggle-tail stallion with the mustang's unnaturally large head bobbing up and down, calling time for a following file of mat-maned, mangy mares. There but for a whim of evolution go I, she opined, as she bade them Godspeed.

On the penultimate day of her journey to Leaning Rock, the trail undertook the mountain pass in all seriousness. Roadside pinones and junipers gradually yielded to the lofty ministry of naked-trunked aspens wearing high, fluttering, marigold-colored bonnets. Eventually the quaking aspens gave way to stands of ponderosas and droopy-branched firs born to shed the snow. All day long she tramped, while the high woods deepened and the soles of her boots depressed spongy, dark mosses. Then with one fell sweep a blanket of darkness covered the woods, giving her no choice except to make her bed on a carpet of leaves and needles. She must have been dog tired, because she fell asleep at once.

When she awoke the sky seemed coldly gray and far, far away. Abruptly, she sensed that somebody or something was looking at her. She held her breath and did not move. Then she heard something, and she knew she was not alone. Daring to take a peek from her blanket, she saw a herd of elk standing as one looking at her. When she pushed the folds of the blanket aside to greet her fellow creatures, they turned and trotted off as if hitched to carts.

Day did not come brightly to the high forest, being known only through random patches of Easter egg blue showing above and beyond the mightiest trees that rarely permitted the companionship of her dearest companion, her shadow. The visits of sunshine became fewer and farther apart as she plodded heavily through soggy earth that smelled stale, as if too long on the shelf. Even the water twinkling through the leafage at the road's edge tasted old. Just the same, it had the virtue of abundance, a capacity ever respected by those disciplined to scarcity.

Holding back, she watched a white tail deer approach the roadside trench in cautious, dandified steps, drink his fill, stand in the water to soothe hoof-line fly bites, then bound away. Seeing the thirst-quenched deer disappear into the dark woods, her thoughts reversed to the antipodal status of the kangaroo rat in the desert below, who had to manufacture his own moisture.

As she trudged on in the perpetual twilight, she didn't seem to have strength of spirit to come to grips with the strange feeling of alienity that permeated her bones as the strange road entered a cloistered, dark woodland where all was loneliness, loneliness that took the form of a demon dogging her tracks, slipping into a mountain cave when she looked back. She wanted to cry—and did.

Before long, however, diagonal shafts of misty light penetrated the dismal overhanging branches, and she was comforted by the notion that the spunky little trail was working itself free from the clutches of gloom. In a little bit the door opened wide, and she joyously emerged upon a slope where random patches of snow lay. But her spirit sagged when she felt the breath of the North Pole, and she had to engage in the awkward business of rearranging her burden so the Two Grey Hills could cloak her body. Then it happened. The high, bright New Mexico sun came forward with a warm welcome, returning her shadow child that had been lost in the deep woods.

Upon observing her shivering frame and her cold wet boots, El Sol turned up its high altitude power to the last notch, and all was well. The equally generous trail then declared a switchback, opening up a rearward vista bearing the triumphant tiding that they were over the hump. What a relief!

The descending trail was not without complications, however. Footage was plagued by ooze from melting snow, causing her to slip a few times—once a half mile drop was thwarted only by a quick grab on to a cotton-fuzzed branch of brinkside apacheplume. Just the same, she couldn't complain, especially after the road began to dry out. After all, the way was not without interludes of healthful inspiration, the roadside often being brightened by the blue-gray tent of spruce, affirming nature's sublime technique for color and line.

Pretty soon, the trail left the abrupt mountain side to weave its way through fairly level stands of timber trees. It paused unexpectedly at a small clearing where, of all things, she came face to face with a row of hollyhocks. Frost shy, their magenta, tissue paper faces cuddled mother-close to the already seeding steeples peeping over a rickrack of rail fence. Some fifty feet back of the enclosure, a trim little log cabin nestled among lodge-pole pines.

21

Carefully observing the cozy little woodland cottage in its rustic setting of dark pines, hollyhocks, and rail fencing, she opined that the tableau would better befit a storybook than a remote mountain pass.

With curiosity licking its chops, she elected to make a friendly, well-mannered overture toward a friendly visit. "Hello!" she greeted. There was no response. And had there been one she probably would have shivered in her boots. Characters in a story book didn't talk back. Obviously the Prince and the Fair Maiden had decamped long ago. The front door was stoutly barriered by a NO TRESPASS warning, and grass was growing all around like nobody had lived there for a long time. Still, somebody had lived there at some time or other, and knowing that made the trail seem less impersonal, less lonely.

As she tramped along, she carried the picture of the quaint cabin, the rail fence, and the flowers with her, meditating upon the probable character and circumstance of former inhabitants. Then just like that, a childhood memory offered its services. It was the home of "The Girl Who Lived on the Mountain." Her mind went back, way, way back.

She told the tale the way it had been.

School had recessed for the summer and it was a boring afternoon. The men had gone back to the field after noon-dinner, Mama was washing the dishes, and Grandma was dozing with her open Bible spread across her chest, her little gold rimmed spectacles pushed back on her gray scraggling hair like some sort of a crown. Despotism seized power. Boldly shaking Granny's spider bed, I demanded, "Wake up, Grandma and tell me a story!"

"Aggravatin' young'un." Mama shook water off her hands, wiping them on her waist apron like she meant business. "If you wake your sick Granny up, you're going to get it, right where it hurts!"

"Hon didn't wake me," Grandma said, "I was just coming to."

Mama shook her head in resignation and went back to the dishpan, "You were snoring!" she muttered.

I edged in close to the bed. "What are you going to tell me today, Granny?"

The old woman, she was forty-eight, pushed the weighty Bible aside and searched among the dusty files of memory. "Would you like to hear the one about the crazy engineer who was going to drive his train to the moon?"

"I've heard that one a hundred times," I said. "I'm sick of it. Tell me something new."

"How about the story of the little lost baby whose clean-picked bones were found in the eagle's nest?"

"I'm sick of that one, too. Tell me one you heard when you were a little girl. They're the best."

Staring into the cobwebby rafters of the dugout ceiling, Grandma's mind went back across the dim hills and valleys of time.

"When I was around your age, I stayed a while at Grandma Ragsdale's when my mama was sick. Granny was quality. She had a fine two-story, white house with double parlors, one for the young folks and company-come, and one for the old folks and the children. There was a wide gallery all the way across the front of the house, and an open breezeway clean through the middle from front to back to let the air through. There were chinaberry trees growing like big umbrellas in the yard, which was pure white sand, and along the walks were rose cuttings growing under up-side-down fruit jars."

Interest was fast growing. "Hurry up Grandma!"

"Well, I was a young'un once myself, and I begged Granny Ragsdale for a story, like you beg me. If I remember rightly, this is one she told me.

"Once upon a time a handsome young bachelor farmer was in love with two girls. One lived in a neat cottage on Clinched Fist mountain and one lived down in Kenshaw Valley in a sort of ramshackle place."

Bug-eyed in anticipation, I nudged close to Grandma's bed. "Go on, Granny."

"Well, this young man would ride his horse up the mountain trail and spark the girl that lived up there, and he would think that for sure she was the one. Then he would go to see the girl who lived in the valley, and he would be just as sure that she was his true love. He just couldn't make up his mind, so he took his problem to his Granny, and asked her how he could tell which one to pop the question to.

"Well, his Granny studied a minute, and then she said, 'Now, Son, you ride down to the house of the girl that lives in the valley and tell her you have a mighty sick horse at your place, and you've heard dough tray scrapings will cure him, and you're wondering whether she could let him have some. Now mind you, if she scrapes some old sour dough off her tray and gives it to you, just thank her and ride on to the girl on the mountain. Any woman that doesn't clean her bread tray after she makes dough would make a lazy wife and a poor housekeeper. If the girl on the mountain gives you some old dough scrapings, too, just thank your stars and look around some more. But I know both girls, and I don't think you'll have to.'

"The boy did what his Granny said. He rode down to the ramshackle house in Kenshaw Valley. The girl came to the door barefooted, with her hair hanging down in her face and one sleeve of her calico dress out at the armhole. He asked her if she could let him have some dough scrapings to cure his sick horse and she said she'd be might glad to. She brought out a case knife and an old wooden tray that was caked an inch thick with sour dough leavings. She scraped off a whole paper pokeful for him. He thanked her and rode off, and when he got out of sight, he threw the sour dough scrapings in some bushes.

"Then the young fellow rode up to the cottage on Clinched Fist Mountain. Everything about the place was neat as a pin. The yard was marked off in flower beds, white dimity curtains were at the windows, and there wasn't a bit of trash laying around anywhere. He knocked at the door and the girl opened it. She had on a clean, freshly-ironed dress, and her hair was neatly curled. She invited him in and he found everything in the house in perfect order. When he asked her if she could spare him some dough tray scrapings for a sick horse, she looked surprised. Then she told him she was sorry, but she scrubbed her dough tray after every baking.

"Well, the boy was on the verge of popping the question right then and there when a funny feeling came over him, like maybe he ought to hold off. So he thanked her and got on his horse and rode back down to the girl in Kenshaw Valley. Two Sundays later they were married by the Church of God preacher."

Feeling shortchanged, I asked Grandma, "What sort of a story is that?" Mama, who was listening in, said, "It's not the way I heard when I was a young'un, but I like it better. It's a true love story." Mama wiped a tear on the corner of her apron.

Before demanding a retelling of the Crazy Engineer to make up for the unsatisfactory love story, I had one more question for Granny, "Did they live happy ever after?"

Grandma signed and looked out of the open dugout door across vast, lonely prairie. "I surmise," she augured, "they had a passel of young'uns and lived from hand to mouth, doing the best they could with what they had to do with. I reckon they got along. They must have had a lot in common."

While the mountain trail proceeded through a tall, but undark forest, memory hopped and skipped from one old scene to another. Soon came a wide clearing domed by azure sky and warmed by ripe sunshine. The field of stumps told a sad tale. Mightiest had been the forest here, and mightiest the devastation.

Axed and sawn, giant ponderosas, hemlocks, and firs had crashed to the earth from whence they had sprung hundreds of years ago. Heads shorn and limbs amputated, bare trunks, went enchained to the sawmill—the sacrificial altar around which industry danced and sang.

The desolate stump fields called to mind the sepulchral bone fields below and to the east on the Staked Plains. Thereabouts, lay scooped-out, old dugouts, where hunters and skinners once slept. In this place civilization's mark was an abandoned log hut. Her human soul forbade entry, so she spread her bed in the dubious shelter of an outside wall of a decrepid cabin, for she was tired. Not only was her body tuckered out, but the weary sun, itself, was asking to be excused.

Feeling the need of a pick-me-up—it had been rather hard day—she fashioned a grate of sorts from small stones, filling it with old chips and twigs. Luckily, she had to sacrifice only one precious match to get a catch. Scooping up a tin cupful of old but clean snow banked up against the north side of the cabin, she brewed a cup of Mormon tea. The warm liquid and a handful of nuts soon eased fatigue's tension, and she turned in. Cuddled in the warm folds of the Two Grey Hills, she lay facing the darkening sky, hoping for eventide communication with the stars. But smoke, clouds, or something kept them away.

Sleep itself stayed away, hiding in the shadows of old stumps, while her agile mind envisioned tomorrow's assemblage at Leaning Rock where the onward pilgrimage to the Fifth Mesa would be organized. She reckoned the initiating group mentioned in the note left by the whirlwind would be on hand early, maybe be there even now, laying the groundwork for the en masse movement.

A feeling of remissness for not being among the first arrivals came over her, but the bluesy feeling evaporated when she began to seriously speculate on various life styles of the other pilgrims. Some would come from other lands, with strange dress and skin of alien pigment. She and they would embrace, for the search for Truth knows no boundaries. Her conjectures had journeyed rather far afield, including the number and sexes of the participating pilgrims, when they were banished by a nibbling, chewing sound a bit too close for comfort. She coughed, and all was silent. She loosened the lid on the menthol jar, and rolled over and went to sleep.

Toward dawn a loose board on the adjacent cabin wall began to flap. In a state of semi-somnambulance, she got up and yanked the board off and went back to bed. When next she awoke, she sat up quickly, attuning her ears to what she thought were the matutinal utterances of her misplaced fellow travelers who had so strangely gone over the hill into infinity that time while she had eaten wild plums.

But she only heard the recitative of the wind, audibly whooshing its way through stumps and seedlings. She quickly surveyed the sky, finding it had a look of milkweed. That wasn't good.

In this season of autumnal equinox, the ever accelerating wind would blow itself out in eight to ten hours. But at this critical stage in her quest, she simply couldn't afford to hole-up that long. She would have to brace herself and take the ill-disposed circumstance in her stride. That's all there was to it.

She washed down a helping of nuts with a cup of cold tea, and then gearing for battle, she marched forth on the final leg of her journey to Leaning Rock.

The climate for travel was just about the worst she had ever encountered, and it was a good thing she had gotten an early start. Strong, chill-laden gusts cut across the land like a heartache, and it seemed that for every forward step she managed to make, she was pushed back a half. For the first hour, maybe an hour and a half, she made miserably poor progress. Then the obliging sun poked its shining orb through the blue-gray, overhead scum, ready for business. Under its salubrious influence, the gale not only renounced something of its sting, but it shifted direction, intersecting the trail west by northwest. By proceeding at an angle, head and shoulders inclined leftward, she was able to fend off the brunt of the storm. This helped a lot.

Pretty soon the trail began to relinquish altitude. Heavy timber thinned out, yielding to fertile vegas abundant in obsequiously bowing grasses, dwarf sunflowers, and roadside asters of Guadalupe blue. Eventually, the only trees left were scrub cedars and pinones, and even these hardy specimens were sparsely settled.

Then it happened. The main Cross Plains Trail that had avoided the mountain pass joined up. She heaved a sigh of relief. The CPT on its circutious round obviously had been coattailed by byroads, logging trails, and cattle paths. Now that its mountain offshoot had returned to the mother root, a worthy avenue of commerce was established.

Wheel-cut ruts were many and deep, although they were stubbornly being reclaimed by original vegetized coverings. Just the same, the indentations were clearly readable. Without doubt, this portion of the Cross Plains Trail had once served as an important wagon and stage route, reawakening in her a latent feeling for historical synthesis. The eye of her mind saw buckskin-clad horsebackers halt, wheel their nags and rein in. She saw covered wagons laden with plain folks and their household plunder slue joltingly to outside ruts and hold back, all giving the right of way and curious eye to the elegant coach with red velvet curtains, all hoping to catch a glimpse of the visitor from that other world, the world of wealth and fashion, the hub and vortex of social and commercial excellence— Kansas City!

The man of the hour, though, was one of their own. Lean, leatherjowled, and cold of eye, his rifle at his side and the taut rawhide lines in his steady hands, he commanded his own world, their world. People hi-signed him and called him "Slim." He was their hero, this antithesis of the dude and the tenderfoot. He was the man in charge of the safety of moving passengers, money and mail, the precursor of the locomotive engineer, and all succeeding men who saw that the goods were delivered. He was the stuff dreams were made of, a rough draft of destiny—the stagecoach driver.

By foolishly allowing herself to become involved with personal irrelevancies, she forgot where she was. Her unguided feet got caught up in runners of devil's claw. She stumbled, but managed not to fall. Her pack did, though, and came open to the devilish delight of the wind that scattered her belongings every which way. By the time she had run everything down and got it back in place, she was out of breath, and, of course she had a coughing spell. When she calmed down she decided it was high time to box straying fancies and bang the lid. The mishap served her right, though, for trying to entice the handsome stagecoach driver.

Setting out again, she wore her face away from the wind, letting her shoulders take the brunt of the gale like a bull in a blizzard. She was thus able to proceed with minimized discomfort. The clumsy posture made for limited vision, but she was able to tell that the trail not only had assumed ever greater dimensions, but had acquired the dignity of escort. Actually double escort, for the road was proceeding midway between parallel rows of bobwar fencing.

Reading upline, cedar posts marched into infinity in the disciplined precision of the telegraph poles that led the railroads across the plains, but at hand, and deprived of the formalism of distance, it was a different story. The supports for the bobwar fence showed pitiable neglect, having declined in standing in direct ratio to the diminishment of essentiality. There was nothing to be kept in or out. In places old staples that once cinched the strands of bobwar to the posts, had flown the coop, leaving rusty, unsupported wire to lose itself in the weeds. Just the same, the depressing scene was not without lighter moments. It was sort of comical to watch an attached post that had broken off from the ground, dance in the wind like a side show puppet.

During lulls, which were coming more often and were of greater duration, she blotted watery eyes on a sleeve and scanned the contiguous area for fellow way-farers heading for Leaning Rock on this important day of assembly that was already nearly half over. Once she thought she saw one wrapped in a gray-green serape, standing under a scrub cedar. She hi-signed brightly but there was no recognition. When she neared the tree, she felt as foolish as all get out for mistaking an upright slab of lichen-covered rock for a person. Just the same, she had a curious inward feeling of relief that it had turned out that way, and she wondered whether on her long, lonely journey she had developed symptoms of that long Greek word for stage fright—the one beginning with "X". Or maybe, closer to home, she simply was self-conscious about her personal appearance. Her cheeks were sunburned, her lips were cracked, and her poor nose was running like a faucet. So maybe it was better that the pilgrim had turned out to be an inanimate hunk of limestone.

She thought of something. Somewhere tucked away in her personal belongings was a perfectly good linen handkerchief, the last of a box of six left among Mama's things. For emotional reasons she decided not to try to get at it unless she saw somebody coming.

The wind became less demanding, and as she followed the haphazardly enclosed road, she indulged in preassessment of the impending experience in the light of immediacy. Back in the old days, better said years, when attainment of her goal lay in the remote, somewhat legendary future, the practical aspects of realization had never come up for serious consideration. They were bridges to be crossed when come to. Now, of course, in a climate of propinquity, it was time to think along concrete lines.

22

Command of the onward march from Leaning Rock to the Fifth Mesa necessarily should be entrusted to a person of unyielding dedication to the search for Truth, a person of sagacity, judicious in action, infinitely patient, and withal possessed with a grace for leadership. Having no comparable prototype, she saw him as a bearded, white-robed Moses leaning on his staff of comfort, his untiring eyes ever alert to the welfare of his flock, his firm but benignant council assistful to all.

It seemed logical that such a leader actually could as well be a woman—except a female Moses wouldn't fit the picture on account of the beard. Anyhow, the person in command probably would take down the names of all the assembled pilgrims and organize them into interdependent units of say a dozen or so. These units then would select group leaders, who in the evenings would supervise sharing of food and philosophies around small, intimate campfires. Preparations for the onward journey to the Fountainhead might well take several days, for the job had to be done right.

In her mind she referred to these units as I.G.'s. These Inspired Groups would discourse far into the night, delving for some mathematical power that would reduce the meaning of Life to comprehensible quantities. Under discussion, which naturally would be heated at times, would be various inquiries such as (A) What is civilization?; (B) What, if anything, is a human being's obligation to society in return for getting born?; (C) Is the concept of God as Lord of Creation brought to this continent by our European forebears more healthful to the human soul than our American Indian's deific absorption of God, nature, man, and fellow creatures into one interrelated, comprehendible whole?

In exploring these ponderables and hypotheses, the I.G.'s might well delve into enigmatic regions beyond the frontiers of human understanding. Life, itself, might come under purview, it being arguable whether Life on earth, i.e. our uniquely evolved existence, really was basic to the vibrating universal system or whether "we" were just a happenstance resulting from some cosmic experiment or accident that our feeble earth-bound intelligence so far, has not been able to savvy.

And she thought how wonderful it will be to participate in discussions with seasoned philosophers, and perhaps even assist in preparation of esoteric data to be weighed on the scales of Truth, readable on the Fifth Mesa!

A strong hairy arm—it looked a lot like Grandpa's—came out of nowhere and motioned, "Slow Down!"

She put the brake on, aware that a small potato like herself, was not eligible to grapple with speculative inquiry beyond her humble sphere of competence. Her attempt to flesh and mind prophets she had never met, or even heard of, except for Moses, was in essence absurd.

Opting for a less recondite frame of mind before family ghosts emerged through the bushes and demanded her committal, she calmly followed the hit-and-miss bobwar strands for a couple of miles or so, when wonderful to behold, the left-hand strand became an adobe wall! Plainly, indubitably, something was coming up. If her intuitive process was in working order, and she would bet a Yankee dime it was, THAT something could be interesting.

In a little bit the ragged old wall spruced up, assuming the stature of a determinant, if caricatural, bulwark of defense. At its height, the courageous old fortification was interrupted by a fairly well-preserved zaguan, solidly spanned, but innocent of gate. Appraising the wagonway, she figured that in its day it could accommodate two vehicles simultaneously or four horsemen abreast—it was that wide. Her whole attention abruptly focused on wooden sign that had dissolved partnership with the gateway, but still in good standing rested on the ground against the wall for all the world to see:

LEANING ROCK LFT. 5 MI.

The interlocking joints of her spine began to shake like snake rattles. She shuddered with chill and then broke out in a sweat. The bald announcement of the real thing an hour's walk ahead had touched off a startling gong.

She sat down on the stone gate prop to assemble her scattered wits. In calmer assessment, she realized that what had happened was no more than the overblown involuntary jump one experiences upon seeing somebody one didn't know was there. She accepted that analogy at face value, but with a personal connotation. She had been caught looking a mess.

Her cheeks were feverish from sunburn, her eyes were watery, and her nose still dripped from blown dust. Her hair was hanging down every which way, and there was dirt under her nails. Somehow, someway, she had to get cleaned up before she joined the other pilgrims. She owed that much to them, to her own sense of personal hygiene, as well as to a proper upbringing that required that she put her best foot forward, especially when walking on historical ground. This, of course, involved water.

Now there was no disputing that this ancient stage stop, fort, or what have you, had been established near a source of water. She simply had to figure out where it was, or had been.

Putting on her thinking cap, the one with the green visor, she reckoned the place might be on the far side of the haphazardly enclosed courtyard. She felt sure of it when with a better view she could see a healthy gathering of cottonwoods standing in steadfast brotherhood against the wind. Their flourishing density not only promised moisture, but a bit of seclusion where she could freshen up, for it would be mighty awkward if she should be turned away by the other pilgrims as an unassimilable entity.

Sighting the sun, she figured if she got a hustle on, she could take time out to clean-up and still make it to Leaning Rock in an hour or two. Hand-toting her pack, she made tracks across the old courtyard, and through an opening on the other side, she beheld something right out of Genesis. Had Adam and Eve started out in New Mexico, as they should have, they would have settled in this vertible Eden. There was no apple tree, but there was a lush wild plum pregnant with little gall bladders of ripe fruits. Pleasureful dwarf sunflowers, butterfly bush, mullien, and sage also lived in complete indifference to wind, whose force was blunted by the cottonwoods.

Presently, she stood in reverence before the time-honored vessel that permitted the caravan to move on—the active, ponderosa-hewn canova. Cupping a palm, she caught drop by accumulated drop of precious cold water as it oozed across a furrowed boulder to fall into the water trough. After lapping well, she dampened her soapweed sponge in the drip-drip and scrubbed her face and hands. The salutary gesture extended to moistening and patting down vagrant wisps of wind-blown hair and dabbing her sun-bronzed cheeks with a bit of face powder she had forgotten she had—an exercise of doubtful cosmetic enhancement, but providing a much-needed feeling of being more socially acceptable.

It was when she stopped to lap a few parting drops to wet her whistle that the whole complexion of things changed. Through a chink in a matted hedge of weed and vine, she caught a glimpse of a house—a very old house.

Obligation to schedule didn't have a chance when up against her native inquisitiveness. After all, an opportunity to explore an old house didn't come along every day. Besides, it would just take a few minutes. It still was early, and although not yet visible, Leaning Rock was but a short walk ahead.

The main entrance to the structure was not immediately visible, being obscured by an expansive clutch of drooping ensiform leaves of an expiring century plant, but she soon made her way to the door, and raising the heavy clapper, let it fall, her muscles recoiling as the sharp rap shocked the deep silence. She listened in tense expectation, almost afraid of what she would hear. But the door remained silent, and the only voice she heard was that of the wind pushing through the cottonwoods.

She knocked again, this time just to make sure. The answer was the cold response of dispeopled desolation. The iron knob was heavy with time and took two hands to turn, but the released door acquiesced without resistance or sound.

She entered. Making her way from room to room, she found nothing of much interest in the debris inside except an old newspaper. She retrieved the paper, blowing off an accumulation of dust, folding the fragile pages so they would fit into a corner of her pack. It would be good to have something to read when she could spare the time. Actually, she hadn't read much of anything except trail signs since her glasses had been broken during a hailstorm she had run into some fifteen miles north of Wagon Mound several years ago. It used to be that she would rather read than eat. Every day she would take along one of the books Dr. Baugh willed to her, especially a volume on history or philosophy, while she herded sheep. But the books were closed now, except to the eye of her mind, and had been for a long, long time.

Back to the present, she noticed an old mirror or picture nailed to a wall. She was about to pass it by when she became aware that whatever it was uttered a message. This development certainly called for more than cursory attention. Devoting a precious moment of unresponsive observation, she decided the ancient, cracked, and blurred looking glass—apparently that's what it was—having no living subject to reflect for many years, had simply lost know-how. But the mirror must have read and disputed her thoughts, because the shadow of a strange face emerged through the vitreous dullness. Quickly, she turned, but no one was there.

Assessing the extraordinary phenomenon, she made the discovery that from a fixed stance the reflection of the face would appear, but upon the slightest shift of an eye, the face erased itself, only to reappear when her eyes assumed key position. It seemed to her as if the eye and the target were in cahoots, and that she was the unwilling participant in some macabre shadow play. With each conjuring up, the face became less strange, more familiar. An unseen hand drew in the straight nose, the deep-set eyes, the thin lips . . .

A chill shuddered her bones. It was her hair. Her hair was sprinkled with ashes!

"No!" her voice echoed in the silence.

Outside again she knew that the wind had allayed. She didn't know when it had stopped. Maybe it just had. All was so still that she could hear the bellows of her own breathing, the beat of her heart. Shouldering the Two Grey Hills, she left the old house, strangely feeling that she was being followed, but when she looked back, no one was there.

In spite of her digression, the afternoon still had far to go. Yet she found herself going lickety split, hurrying away from more than toward. Pretty soon breathing began to labor and she had to stop and cough. This was not good, and her native good sense came to her rescue. Shedding her pack, she sat down on a roadside rock, drank from the canteen, and assessed her situation, coming to the conclusion that her nerves had gotten shook up a bit due to (A) Leaning Rock being nowhere in sight, and invisibility being connotative of nonexistence, and (B) the cracked mirror incident. Small wonder she was as nervous as a cat. A combination of frustrations like that would make even Hawthorne's Great Stone Face wince. Nothing to be upset about at all.

Calmed down and on the road again, her long, hard legs settled down to their normal stride of four point three miles an hour, although before she had pneumonia, she could maintain half-again that rate.

The trail's legend narrowed mile by mile, yet Leaning Rock still hid its face, but she took its invisibility in her stride, pausing only to snare and despine ripe prickly pears, which she pocketed to share with others.

Before long the trail undertook an increasingly barren area. Sickle-bladed gramma, russet-leafed scrub oaks, and stunted cedars phased into mesquite, sage, and cholla as the indomitable desert assumed control. The monstrous eye of the bloated sun glared mercilessly on the arid earth, and beads of sweat broke out on her forehead, the saline secretion saturating her clothing with embarrassing body wetness.

She kept an eye out for a community of wild gourds so she could fashion a fan from their broad leaves, but none appeared. Even the toughest vegetations, sage and snakeweed, were in scant supply. They, too, soon disappeared.

Bereft of growing things, the road drew its lonely track across barren terrain inhabited by curious earth formations, dikes, pinnacles, tepees with hats on, chimneys, and cathedrals, all established at eye level against a mauve-rose sky. Plagued by the eerie feeling that she was being taken on a detour through some sort of mythological underworld, she quickened her steps to get shed of it.

Suddenly she saw it. Cold shivers halted the flow of sweat. There it stood! Unbelievably, there it stood, its great petrous shoulder bowing across a vast flow of amber-colored earth in homage to a declining sun. Her human soul overflowed with gratitude and humility, and her eyes wanted to mist, but there was no time for emotional indulgence. She must get to the haven of the rock as quickly as possible.

On that last half mile, the trail pursued the east-flowing shadow of the monument, and an aura of solemnity pervaded her human soul. Over the years, and they had been many, when awarded a glimpse of Leaning Rock, it had looked like a great axe-head driven aslant into the earth by some preternatural force. Now, at hand, so near her feet trod its far-flung shadow, it didn't look like an axe-head at all, but more like a tombstone. Sometimes in desolate graveyards, especially in the country, you'd see a headstone of immodest proportions sagging awry in the loose soil, and you'd speculate upon what moment of what hour of what day of what year of what century it would topple.

Maybe the analogy was there, but she shooed the mental insinuation away. This was no time for becoming involved with those kinds of thoughts. Anyway, the trail was now veering away from the great rock's lugubrious shadow to approach from the south, still sunlit.

In the saffron-yellow light of the lowering sun, she joyously descried at the rock's base the figures of many persons. Clasping the burden of her travels to her breast so it wouldn't bob up and down on her back, she ran.

23

But when panting for breath she arrived at the landmark's base, no one was there. Not a soul. Nothing except gray-robed silence. Coming to grips with reality, having been deceived so many times before, she knew the answer. The illusory rays of the lowering sun had distorted the tumbleweeds that had sprung up in the moist earth in the vicinity of a pool at the base of the rock, making them look like persons.

She was downright chagrinned by the realization that again she had been tooken by an optical illusion, and she decided not to tell anybody when the pilgrims arrived. Some of them ought to be coming long any time now. As a friendly gesture of welcome, she decided to station herself where she could wave any of the pilgrims on. Clambering to the top of nearby boulder, she eagerly surveyed all avenues of approach, but there was no sound or sign of life. Discouraged, she got down.

A feeling of apprehension tried to surface, but she reproved it, suggesting that the other pilgrims probably had been delayed by the same windstorm that had retarded her own progress. Fortunately, she had been able to transit a relatively dust free, vegetized area during storm's high fever. Those proceeding from the valley would have been deterred by low visibility. It was safe to assume that they had taken cover at the height of the gale, and now that it had blown itself out, would be arriving pretty soon. It would be light enough for travel for another hour, give or take a few minutes. Moreover, with a good moon and a cloudless sky, they might come straggling in throughout the night.

In a way, she was glad that she had been the first to arrive. She had never been what one might call, "socially turned." One thing that had bothered her on this simpatico day was whether her native shyness in the presence of strangers might prejudice assimilation. Being first on the scene, however, she would be cast in the role of hostess, obviating the inglorious chance of being overlooked. Moreover, thanks to the pool's benificence, she would have an opportunity to wash up. Those last few miles had been hot and dusty.

Only a hop, skip, and a jump from the mirror-clear pool she espied a concave accessory basin obviously hollowed by years of overhead drain. At the moment the depression was as dry as a bone, and probably had been for many a day. In recognition of its utilitarian aspects, however, some thoughtful prior sojourner had sunk a hook in the adjacent rock wall and hung a reamed gourd dipper.

The decrepit dipper was about as continent as a cracked egg shell, making the chore of filling the birdbath-size hollow an uneasy one. Just the same, by industrious manipulation, she was able to outrun leakage until the receptacle was adequately supplied with clean water, although in the process she slipped several times, once coming within an ace of falling into the pool.

Checking behind boulders and examining pool-nourished tumbleweeds and yuccas to make sure she was alone, she divested her clothing. A looksee into the reflection on the smooth surface of the pool was shocking, even frightening. Her skinny old body was bicolored. The torso was as pale and skeletal as a white ant, while the rest of her body, the parts long explosed to the high, bright New Mexico sun, were the color of sorghum molasses. With more pathos than amusement, she reckoned she must look like some old broken-down pinto mare ready for that last roundup. But there was no time for getting all bluesy. That would have to wait for some sleepless, lonely night.

Testing the water in the half-filled basin with an out-turned toe, she shrank from the chill and she questioned whether she ought to go ahead with a bath that just might bring her down with a cold. But memory conjured Granny down from the sky and the matter was left to her. The answer, of course, was "Cleanliness is next to Godliness."

A scrawny, self-conscious, parti-colored Eve stood shivering in the little stone tub while her bony fingers kneaded the moist, self-contained soapweed sponge into a lather. Beginning at the top, she progressed downward. With the exception of her feet, she submitted her epidermal surface, even places having only a nodding acquaintance with cleansing agents, to an almost brutal scrubbing. According to New Mexico's pan-bathing tradition, the feet came last. Playfully rubbing the dirt off each other, they splashed coffee-colored water every which way, like robins in a puddle, and she reckoned that even if she caught a cold the bath was worth it.

She left her boots off when she dressed. They needed to air out. Barefooted and light hearted as a gypsy, she fluttered about, tidying the place up. Using a dried yucca stalk as a broom of sorts, she swept aside animal droppings, bits of caught paper, and weed chaff. Next, she laid out her food supply in orderly placement on the smooth surface of a natural stone table.

In this season of maturity, she had a good batch of seeds and nuts, in addition to the packet of jerky she long had toted as an emergency ration. From the smell, she wondered whether the carne seca had soured or something. When she pulled the casing off there weren't any maggots, and really the stuff looked better than it smelled. So she figured what the jerky needed was explosure to New Mexico's revivifying air and sun. She laid it out on a rock that still caught the sun, thinking that perhaps someone less vegetarian than she might find it palatable. Lastly, she pridefully flung the gonfalon of her estate across a prominent boulder where all the world could see. Not everyone owned a Two Grey Hills.

With everything shipshape, and herself feeling clean as a whistle, groomed and ready, except for her boots which still were airing, she sat down for a bit of rest, occupying a stool-size rock where her eager eyes could keep watch over the trail.

To make the interval before the arrival of other pilgrims less long, she gave favored position to speculation, with which she was abundantly endowed. In the first place, she wondered how it had come to pass that an alien rock, a pool, and plant life should inhabit this barren, erosional spot. Then, reversing the lens in the glass of time, she looked back thousands and thousands of years. The ground heaved and shook, and she swayed with it. Then, from deep in the guts of the earth came awful grunts and rumblings. Something popped. With a violent cataclysm that was heard and felt all over the southwest, a Jemez mountain erupted, ejecting great molten bubbles that fell back to embed themselves into the red earth's crust, creating the Valle Grande caldera, one of the widest on the globe. In the process, an eccentric projectile, plowing across the sky in a cloud of steam, headed this way. In wide-eyed wonder, she watched a flaming arrowhead soar, and then fall to plunge its triangonal blade into the tight red earth, sinking its shaft to the hilt, puncturing a subterranean artery that hemorrhaged for a thousand years as the scorch cooled, then slowly the seepage from the wound surfaced, creating an eternal fountain in a waterless land.

What a magnificent gesture, and how fitting that the pilgrimage to the Fifth Mesa should set forth from this wonderously contrived oasis! How splendid that she should live to . . .

Something that looked like an enormous black leaf, was gliding downward across the inclined rock wall.

It wasn't a leaf!

Mystified, she watched the descent of a large, dark bird. Presuming the creature wanted to drink, she moved well away from the perimeter of the pool. Oddly, disturbingly, the bird skipped the surface of the pool, heading in her direction, coming in so close she could hear the whirr of its wings. She quickly side-stepped and the bird flapped past.

An unnatural atmosphere of impending insecurity flowed in like sudden smoke. She was baffled, heartsick, and afraid. So help her Hannah, in all her long years of pilgrimage she always had enjoyed good rapport with fellow creatures— except, of course, the time she had sunk bare foot into a boot where a scorpion was sleeping, and that was an accident.

"Oh, my God!" she cried. "Here it comes again!"

Seizing the Two Grey Hills, she flailed the bird off knowing it would be back. An appetite so voraciously whetted would not give up. While it calculated reapproach, she leaned against the rock and coughed and coughed. Again it came, and again its purpose was deflected, but in the heated exercise, the blanket swerved against the surface of the pool, splashing water all over the place. Her bare feet slipped on the grimy slosh, and waving her arms like a rope dancer, she skidded right down to the water's edge, coming within an ace of falling in.

Fraught with mingled anger and trepidation, she wondered what heinous force had taken possession of her dignity, hanging the albatross of fear around her neck. What strange fruit had she fed upon to change a conscious human being into a trembling rabbit?

"Devil!" she cried out, as she watched the bird's return.

The cord snapped, like one's outcry breaks the hold of a tormenting dream. Smoothing herself out, she watched it come in with the casual interest of one watching a sparrow sneak up for a crumb.

This time the predator approached in cautious stealth, keeping away from where she now stood in calm self-confidence. With a well-calculated drop of raptorial talons, it lit, and savagely tore up and devoured the rasher of jerky. Then, stretching its wings, bowing and defecating, it took to air, not to return.

As if nothing had happened, a capricious breeze fooled around with unfixed wisps of hair. Sighing heavily, she smoothed the loose strands back from her perspiring forehead and surveyed the mess stirred up by the ridiculous skirmish with the starving vulture or whatever it was—it didn't have the usual red wattles. But there was no time for going into the ins and outs of what it was, or, more importantly, why she handled the situation so poorly. She only knew that ever since she had looked in that awful mirror, she hadn't been herself.

Be that as it may, the first thing she had to do, and do quickly, was to clean up the place. She certainly did not want any of her fellow pilgrims to walk in on such a litter of nuts, seeds, feathers, mud, bird manure, and scattered personal belongings. Her old pocket knife, actually it was Virgil's but he couldn't find it when he left, lay perilously close to the edge of the pool. Quickly retrieving it, she rescued her comb, the menthol jar, and her purse containing two five cent pieces and a copper, all of which she returned to proper residence.

When order had been more or less restored and the Two Grey Hills had been rehung to dry, she sought to calm down and assemble her wits, which had taken off in all directions. She felt that she would be all right if she could just get warm. Moving into a shadowless area still under the influence of the departing sun, she fluttered her damp skirts in the manner of a hen fluffing dust. In a little bit they were dry, or nearly so, and she felt okay.

She was surprised to see a folded newspaper lying calmly on a shelf of rock on the far side of the pool. In all the hubub and confusion, she had forgotten all about the old paper she had picked up back at the old house. She supposed that it had been splashed and ruined, but upon examination she found that the paper had survived the fracas with small loss of essential texturing. She sat down at the side of the pool that still caught the waning light and began thumbing through the spread pages, thinking the while that if any pilgrims planned to arrive by daylight, they had better begin showing up, for there was barely enough light for her to make out the print. Even so, a small item leaped to her attention:

QUAY COUNTY ITEMS OF INTEREST

Murdock, Sept. 25 — Some half a hundred members of a religious sect moving from their Pecos Valley farms passed through this community today on their way to Leaning Rock. Their leader, Rev. Erasmus Judd, said they expect to arrive at the rock by the weekend and join up with fellow members from Ragland, Melrose, and LaLande. Rev. Judd said the group would camp at Leaning Rock until organized to proceed en masse on a Revelatory Journey to a mysterious plateau where they believe life's innermost secrets will be revealed.

——————— ——————— ———————

A prominent Quay County rancher, Thomas F. Irving died . . .

Her eyes quickly sought the masthead of the Tucumcari Star. The issue was fifty years old!

She sat still for a few moments, then, folding the fragile pages, she put the old newspaper aside. She would use it to start a fire to brew herself a good cup of Mormon tea. She sure needed it.

She was reminded of something! She had not laid eyes on her boots since the skirmish. The last time she saw them they were sitting side by side near the brink of the pool. She searched everywhere, even among the tumbleweeds, putting off looking where she feared they would be until all less disquieting alternatives had been exhausted. Finally, coming to grips with reality, she knelt, peering into the silent, undiffused water. They were there all right, resting on their sides at the bottom of the pool, far, far out of reach.

She was tired. It hadn't been what one would call an easy day. She ought to start picking out a place to spread her bed. But when she started to leave the pool, something drew her back. It was a retelling of the tale told by the decrepit old mirror. Patiently and without trepidation, she studied the reflected image. There really were ashes in her hair. Not only that, but her cheeks were sunken, and crow's tracks were at the corners of her mouth.

Somehow, it no longer mattered. Not much anyhow. Funny thing, if she had not known better she would have sworn the face in the pool was Mama's—the way she looked lying there . . . Oh, well, with so much to be done it was better not to think about it.

Far enough away from the water hole so animals could come to drink undisturbed, she staked out a circular stand of yucca that would provide a suitable bedroom. Nearby was a huddle of small stones, a grill of sorts, left by an erstwhile camper. Crushing the brittle old newspaper, she laid it among the stones, covering it with dry weeds and pellets of sheep waste. Risking one of her precious matches, she ignited the farolito, the little shepherd's fire that would heat a tin of water for her tea and at the same time signal the way of some lonely wayfarer seeking his spiritual home.

In a parting gesture, the lowering sun steeped the western sky in a curious apricot haze that came right down to the earth's tight rim, where amethyst cathedrals with whimsically crocheted spires, giant toadstools, and great index fingers stood out in never-never perspective. Overhead, the towering, grizzly rock leaned to whisper petrous secrets to the shadows, while the valiant shepherd's fire, smiling to the very end, flickered out, leaving a pervasive redolence of animal midden.

When the last drop of tea was drunk and the sky was beginning to darken, she spread the Two Grey Hills among the yucca. Too keyed up to get to sleep right away, she sought relaxation in communication with her dear friends, the emerging stars. But somehow the interlude lacked inspiration. It seemed as if the whole celestial family was as pooped as she. Even the proud symbol of harvest seemed to drowse in a gold wire hammock.

Leaning on an elbow, she switched range, re-exploring the western horizon, hoping the pearly twilight would reveal boundaries of certain cherished monuments—one, especially, the one she needed most right now. But the west was swathed in slate-blue vapor. Settling down, closing her eyes, her unsmiling thoughts rambled through many things, including the irreducible sovereignty of Time, preordained since creation. All living things under its autocratic sway were sentenced to death at the moment of birth. It was just a matter of Time. Time held the stop watch.

The melancholy contemplations were interrupted when her curtained eyeballs registered a sudden moment of illumination, as if a guiding beacon had swung past. In a few seconds the rumble of the wheels of the tater wagon startled the silent earth. She sat up quickly. A second flash revealed and erased a billow of deep blue cloud lined with rose. This portenous moment breathed strength into her sagging spirits. Tense, daring to hope, she awaited further revelation.

Then came another flash, this one lighting up the entire area, giving an unholy moment of day to the massive rock, the eerie limestone pinnacles, the brown tumbleweeds. Some distance ahead the four purple guardian mesas stood out in bold relief, as if just created and placed on display by a master stonemason. The moment of illumination was so nimble she couldn't be sure, but she thought something shimmered in the background like a curtain of watered silk.

While listening to the wheels of the tater wagon jolt over the earth and away, she counted the seconds. Another flash would come quickly, if at all. On the stroke of five, the shutter opened and closed. But in that magic moment she looked upon a tableland of dove-white marble, lovely and serene as a cameo, so exalted as to assure TRUTH.

Unscrewing the lid on the menthol jar, awakening its potence with a forefinger, she carefully snugged it under the ensiform leaves of yucca, from whose stout fibers she would begin weaving sandals at dawn.

At peace now, she settled down and drew the soft curtain of eventide over her tired eyes. And the slumbrous improvisations of the night wind of the desert became fainter . . . . . and fainter . . . . . .

THE END

www.ingramcontent.com/pod-product-compliance
Lightning Source LLC
Chambersburg PA
CBHW022141020726
47496CB00008B/2501